THE LOST BOOK TRILOGY

the book of
secrets

D0864709

KATHY LEE

© Kathy Lee
First published 2008, Reprinted 2009
ISBN 978 1 84427 342 3

Scripture Union
207–209 Queensway, Bletchley, Milton Keynes, MK2 2EB, England
Email: info@scriptureunion.org.uk
Website: www.scriptureunion.org.uk

Scripture Union Australia
Locked Bag 2, Central Coast Business Centre, NSW 2252
Website: www.scriptureunion.org.au

Scripture Union USA
PO Box 987, Valley Forge, PA 19482
Website: www.scriptureunion.org

British Library Cataloguing-in-Publication Data.
A catalogue record of this book is available from the British Library.

Printed and bound in India by Thomson Press India Ltd

Cover design: GoBallistic
Internal design and page layout: Author and Publisher Services

  Scripture Union is an international Christian charity working with churches in more than 130 countries, providing resources to bring the good news about Jesus Christ to children, young people and families and to encourage them to develop spiritually through the Bible and prayer.

As well as our network of volunteers, staff and associates who run holidays, church-based events and school Christian groups, we produce a wide range of publications and support those who use our resources through training programmes.

1
The boat

The sky was almost as black as night, and the wind was ferocious.

We had lowered the sails. At least that stopped the boat from capsizing, and the sails from being ripped away. But, without sails, the steering gear was useless. The wind and the waves could take us wherever they wanted.

And those waves were getting bigger, coming in from the west with the storm. They were huge and grey, like moving mountains. They would sweep us eastwards, towards the land.

In a storm, land doesn't mean safety. It can mean getting smashed against rocks. The sea and the land can crush a boat, like grain being crushed between two millstones.

And we were drifting helplessly, closer and closer.

Rob's face was pale. He looked scared and seasick. "Maybe it's true," he muttered. "Maybe the boat *is* unlucky."

Yes. If only we'd never touched it... If only we'd left it alone, the sea would have taken it away again. And we wouldn't be here now. We would be safe at home, with the shutters fastened against the wind and the rain.

The mysterious boat had appeared one day on the shore of Insh More, our island. There had been a storm, and Dad had sent us out to rake up seaweed for the fields. We went out eagerly. You never knew what might be washed up on the shore after a storm.

My friend Rob was with me. I think he was the one who saw it first. It lay like a pale rock, half-covered in seaweed. But it wasn't a rock. It was smooth to touch and slippery like a fish. And its shape was obvious – a boat, an upturned boat.

But I'd never seen a boat like this. It wasn't built of wooden planks, like our small fishing boat. The hull was all in one piece, smooth as an eggshell. And, when we lifted one side, it wasn't heavy. We could easily turn it over.

When it was the right way up, we had a good look at it. There were seats along each side, made from the same stuff as the hull. No mast, just a gap where a mast would have fitted, long ago. And it was twice the size of our one-sailed wooden boat.

Very strange. How had this boat ended up on our shore?

"The storm brought it," said Rob.

"Where from?" I said.

"From long ago. From the time of the Ancestors."

"Shhh!" It was unlucky to talk about the Ancestors. Everyone knew that.

"What's that you've found?" Grandad shouted.

He had arrived with the cart to pick up our seaweed. But so far we hadn't collected any. We'd been too busy looking at our find.

Grandad was very interested in the strange boat. He tapped the side of it, and the noise was not like wood or metal, but soft and muffled. And yet the boat itself wasn't soft. It was quite strong. It must be, if it had survived from the time of the Ancestors.

"What's it made of, Grandad?" I asked him.

"I don't know. Plastic, maybe?"

I knew what plastic was. Every now and then plastic bottles would get washed up on the shore. The Ancestors must have made thousands of them. They didn't rust like iron, or rot like wood, or crack like pottery. They were everlasting.

The boat was made of similar stuff, but it was greyish-coloured, not see-through. It would last far longer than a normal wooden boat. Grandad saw its possibilities at once.

"I could maybe make a mast for it," he said. "And a sail."

"You'd need a rudder to steer it with," said Rob.

"Mmm." He looked at it thoughtfully. "It could make a good fishing boat. Pull it up above the tide line."

During that winter, Grandad spent a lot of time working on the boat. I helped him whenever I could. The short daylight hours didn't leave much time after I finished my work, helping Dad with the cattle and sheep.

I didn't like the winter. There was never enough light or warmth. Not enough food sometimes too. And that winter was a bad one.

Storm after storm swept in from the sea, so that fishing was impossible. And, in between the storms, it seemed to rain non-stop. Our store of potatoes caught some disease that made them turn mouldy. A wild dog appeared on the island – people said it must have swum over from the mainland – and started killing sheep.

The dog was the worst problem. We couldn't leave it to run wild and kill sheep whenever it was hungry. Everyone on the island got together to hunt it down.

At the gathering, Rob's father, the chief of Insh More, organised us into a long line and made sure we all had weapons. I had my bow and arrows. Rob had a dagger. We looked enviously at his three big brothers, who each had a sword.

We worked our way up the hill. When we were nearly at the top, all our dogs began to bark. The wild dog appeared on the skyline. Instantly, I had an arrow on the bowstring, but I couldn't shoot for fear of hitting one of our own dogs.

Swiftly the dogs hunted down the enemy who had invaded their island. By the time we caught up with them, there was no need for swords or arrows. The wild dog was dead.

We hauled our dogs off before they started to fight each other. Rob's father held up the mangled body of the sheep-killer, and everybody cheered. But it was a half-hearted sort of cheer. And by now I'd noticed something.

People were avoiding my family. Nobody wanted to speak to Grandad or Dad or me. What was the matter? It wasn't our dog that had run wild, although the wild dog had been living on our side of the hill.

When Grandad invited people back to our house to celebrate the day's hunting, people made excuses. Too much work to do or a sick cow to see to... It was odd. Normally everyone loved a celebration. It brightened up the dark winter days.

"What's the matter with all of you?" Grandad said, bewildered.

At first nobody answered. Then Angus, our nearest neighbour, spoke up.

"You're bringing bad luck on the island," he said. "That boat – you should never have touched it."

Other people agreed. "This is the worst winter in years. And it's all because of you and that boat. Put it back in the sea and let it go!"

"No," said Grandad, stubbornly. "When I've finished, it'll be the best boat on the island. There's nothing wrong with it at all!"

"Nothing wrong with it? It's unlucky!" they added. "It'll be the death of you. And maybe all of us."

"Do you want to make the sea rise up again?" Angus asked.

People crowded round, looking angry. But then Rob's father broke in. He was the chief – it was his job to settle arguments and keep the peace.

"Angus, Angus. If everything from the Old Times is unlucky, why are you still using that water tank of yours? Maisie, your copper pans that you're so proud of – they must be unlucky too. And what about me? I'm living in a house from the Old Times! Am I bringing bad luck on the island?"

He turned to Grandad. "I say you can carry on with your boat. And, if it brings bad luck with it, let it be on your own head and nobody else's."

I looked around the circle of faces. They would go along with what the chief said, but they didn't like it; I could tell.

And they were right – the boat did bring bad luck. I wish Grandad had listened.

2
The first trip

My name is James, but most people call me Jamie. In the year when we found the boat, I was 11 years old.

I was born on the island of Insh More. My home was a small house, roofed with peat and walled with stone. Grandad's grandfather built it using stones from another house, lower down, which was being swallowed up by the sea.

My mother died when I was very young. She took a fever and died just a few days after my sister was born. I don't remember her – I don't even know what she looked like.

It was Granny who took care of Elspeth and me, while Dad and Grandad shared the work of farming and fishing. As soon as we were old enough, we learned to help them. I can't remember a time when I didn't know how to gut fish, mend nets or herd sheep.

Apart from a few visits to the town on the mainland, I'd never been anywhere except the island. People say that it was once joined on to the mainland, long ago before the sea rose up. In the Old Times it was all part of a country called Scotland. But now the sea has divided that land into many islands – some big, some small.

It was the Ancestors who made the sea rise. They didn't mean to do it, so people say. (I've heard this story ever since I was a baby. The tale of the Ancestors is told once a year, on the darkest night of the winter, so that no one makes the same mistake again.)

The Ancestors were very clever, but also stupid. They were clever enough to find a way of flying through the air. They knew how to make water come out of pipes in the wall, instead of having to be fetched from rivers and wells. (It's true. I've seen the places where this used to happen in the big house where Rob lives.) They could cure all kinds of sickness. They could speak to people far away. They had music that played itself and food that cooked itself, and all kinds of amazing knowledge – if you believe the old tales.

But they were foolish too. They didn't know that they were making the world heat up, with all their machines working away. Or, if they knew, they didn't care. Not until it was too late.

Then the world became so warm that ice in the far north began to melt. And slowly, the seas began to rise. This was in the time of my great-great-great-great-great grandfather.

The Ancestors mostly lived on low-lying land, in great cities – far bigger than our town and so big that you couldn't count how many people lived there. The Ancestors tried to keep the sea out of their cities, but it was too strong for them. And it went on rising, turning farmland to salt marsh, hills to islands, and great cities to flooded ruins.

For all their cleverness, most of the Ancestors didn't know how to live off the land. They had no idea how to plant crops or raise animals. They didn't die from drowning, but from hunger and thirst. And still the sea was rising.

In the time of my great-great grandfather, there weren't many survivors. As the sea rose and the land shrank, there was only enough farmland for a few people to live on. It was hill country, stony and rough. All the best land was under the sea.

By the time Grandad was born, the sea had stopped rising. People had managed to survive, but the clever ways of the Ancestors were mostly forgotten. "And a good thing too," Granny always said, as she ended the tale.

Grandad didn't agree with her. He thought it was a pity that so much knowledge had been lost. For instance, he wanted to know how to rig the Ancestors' boat. He thought it had been built to have a single mast, but two sails. It would have needed two people to control it – one steering, one handling the sails.

The mast had probably been made of metal. In the Old Times, people say, there was plenty of metal, but now it's scarce and valuable. So Grandad made a mast of wood and a wooden rudder that fitted the empty slots at the stern. The sails were cut from hemp cloth, like the sail of our old fishing boat, but bigger.

By early spring, he was ready to try out the boat. He didn't want lots of people watching, in case it all went wrong. Of course, people knew what he was doing, but most of them kept well away. Only my family knew how the boat was coming on.

And Rob knew, of course. Rob wasn't frightened by the talk of bad luck. He was interested in the Ancestors, always wanting to find out more about them. He gave us quite a bit of help with the boat.

One day, when the wind was light but steady and the sea was fairly calm, Grandad announced that we were ready to make our first trip.

Watched by Dad, Granny and Elspeth, the three of us dragged the boat down to the water. We climbed on board and hauled in the slack sails. At once, the boat seemed to leap into life.

Faster and faster, with a white wake behind us, we sailed out into the bay. And this was in a light wind! What would the boat do if the wind picked up?

"Hey! This is great!" shouted Rob.

"You were right, Grandad. The best boat on the island!" I told him.

Grandad's wrinkled face was full of smiles. All our work had paid off, and he had been proved right. And I think he loved the boat. He had forgotten where it came from – it was his boat now.

In the next few days, we learned the best way to handle it. How to tack, heading into the wind. How to haul in the small sail and dodge the mainsail boom as it swung across. How to make sure our weight was in the right place to balance the boat when the wind made it heel over.

Then we went on our first fishing trip. It was a good one. We brought back twice as much fish as our old boat used to carry. That was the end of the winter food shortage. Everyone had as much fish as they could eat, and the rest of the catch was smoked so that it would keep for later.

As the fishing season went on, people stopped talking about bad luck. Instead, they tried to sail after us so that they could fish where we fished. Grandad enjoyed watching them get left behind.

Sometimes we fished out at sea, around rocky isles that were the tops of drowned hills. Other times we sailed up and down the mainland coast. But always we had to keep an eye to the west, looking out for a storm on the way. Even in summer, storms could brew up so quickly that it was frightening.

Whenever he could, Rob came with us. He was bored with the life of a chief's son. Except for sword-fighting, which he loved, everything he had to learn seemed pointless. He was the youngest of four brothers (all tall, red-haired and freckle-faced, like himself), so it wasn't likely he would ever be chief. As for reading and writing, what was the good of it? Much better to learn something useful, like fishing.

And so Rob was with us on that terrible day – the day of the great storm.

3
The storm

There are more storms now than in the Old Times – that's what people say. It's all because of the world warming up. The storms are fiercer and more sudden. (I wonder if the Ancestors were clever enough to know when a storm was on its way. They couldn't do the really clever thing, though – they couldn't stop it from happening.)

The day before the great storm the weather was fine, with a steady wind. We sailed a long way south. There was a rocky headland on the horizon – you could see it from the island. To me, it was like the southern edge of the world. But, that day, we sailed beyond it.

Rob was excited as we rounded the headland. I wondered what he expected to find. A new stretch of coastline opened out in front of us. But it was much the same as before – hills, lonely islands, endless grey sea.

"I thought we might see the land of Lothian," he said, disappointed.

Grandad laughed. "You'd have to go a lot further south for that. South and east. A week or more, it would take, even if the wind was right."

Lothian! I'd heard the name, of course. People talked about it almost like a land in a story.

In Lothian, they said, there was a king living in a great castle surrounded by the sea. His city, Embra, was a place of marvels. The buildings were as tall as trees. The harbour was crowded with boats. And the streets were full of people: buying and selling things, begging, playing music, stealing food...

"I saw more people there in one day than I'd ever seen in the whole of my life," Rob's uncle always said. He had actually travelled to Embra, years ago, when he was young and adventurous. He had fought in the king's army, and helped to defeat the Norse raiders. The stories of what he had done in Lothian got better with each telling.

Rob was longing to go there. He said we could both go, when we were a bit older. Sometimes I wanted to – especially in winter, when life on the island was empty and bleak.

But it was summer now, and there were fish in the water, waiting to be caught. We got to work and forgot about strange, faraway places.

On our first few tries, we didn't catch much. We sailed closer to the shore and put the net out again. And this was when the bad luck began. The net got caught on something under the water. We went round and round, trying to free it, without success.

The net was valuable. It would take weeks of work to make another one. So Rob and I tried swimming underwater, following the rope downwards. We were both good swimmers, unlike Grandad. (When he was young, nobody learned to swim. People thought of the sea as their enemy then, and learning to swim was unlucky.)

It was no use – the rope went down deeper than we could swim. But the tide was going out. If we waited until the water was shallower, we might be able to get our net back.

In the late afternoon we went swimming again. And this time things went better. I couldn't see much underwater, but I could feel the thing that had caught our net. It was made of metal, all crusted with sea shells and coral.

My lungs were bursting. I went up for more air, then dived down again. Carefully I tugged at the net, sliding it up and over the metal thing, until at last it was free.

Grandad was pleased. "Well done, Jamie. What was it caught on? A rock?"

"No, it felt like metal. Like one of the metal towers from the Old Times." The Ancestors had built those weird-looking towers in a long line, like six-armed giants striding over hills and valleys. No one knew why.

I shivered slightly as I dried myself off. I felt it was unlucky that something from the Old Times had reached

out to grab us, like a hand reaching up from the seabed...
And another unlucky thing – the wind had dropped.

"Will we have to row all the way back?" asked Rob.

Grandad had made a couple of oars for the boat, but
rowing it was hard work. It wasn't the right shape for a
rowing boat; it was awkward and slow. And we had
come a long way from home.

"Even if we row like mad, we won't get back before
dark," I said.

Grandad agreed. "We'd better find someplace to stay
the night, and hope for a bit of wind in the morning."

We rowed as far as a small island. (Somehow an
island felt safer than an unknown part of the mainland.)
We made a fire out of driftwood and cooked ourselves
some fish. It was a warm night, and soon I fell asleep
under the stars.

Next thing I knew, Grandad was shaking me awake.

"Come on, Jamie – wake up! I don't like the look of
the weather."

The sun was just rising, but in the west there was a
huge wall of dark clouds. The wind was blowing in short,
sharp gusts. The sea was full of angry-looking waves.

A storm was on the way – anyone could see that. And
there was no shelter on our tiny island. It was so low and
flat that storm-waves might sweep right over it.

Quickly we launched the boat. We had to head
westwards, tacking into the wind, to get around the long

headland that cut us off from home. It was hard work. The wind was so gusty that it almost capsized us a couple of times.

Rounding the headland, we still had a long way to go. I could see our island, far to the north, each time a wave lifted us up.

The black clouds had covered most of the sky by now. Each wave that came in seemed bigger than the last. Grandad was having trouble steering in a straight line. The wind and the waves were sweeping us off course, towards the mainland.

Grandad kept looking anxiously at the mainsail. The wind would stretch it as tight as a bowstring, then suddenly ease off and leave it flapping about. When the sail was tight, Rob and I had to lean right out over the side, to balance the boat.

It was frightening. Even Grandad was scared; I could tell. And I'd never seen him scared before.

Rob said, "Why don't we just make for the nearest shore?"

"Because I don't want the boat to get smashed up on the rocks," Grandad said through gritted teeth.

He was still steering for the island. It had a sheltered bay with a sloping shore where we might be able to land safely, even in the storm. But it was still a long way off, and we were being blown sideways, towards the mainland.

Another huge gust of wind hit us. The sails weren't built for this! Any minute now, they could rip away from the ropes that held them.

"Lower the sails," Grandad ordered.

"What?"

"You heard me. Lower the sails. Maybe we can sit out the worst of the storm here, well away from the land."

But his plan didn't work. Even without sails, we were still being carried eastward by waves that were almost mast-high. I couldn't believe the size of them. The boat heaved up to the crest of each wave, then plunged into the deep hollow beyond. Again... again... again...

My stomach lurched. I wanted to be sick. I'd never been seasick in my life. But then I'd never been at sea in a storm.

Grandad shouted something, but I couldn't hear him above the howling of the wind.

"The oars!" Rob yelled in my ear.

We got the oars out and struggled to row the boat away from the land. It was impossible, with the wind and the sea against us. The mainland hills were looming closer all the time.

"We'll have to look for someplace to land!" Grandad yelled.

My heart sank even further. We didn't know this part of the coast. It looked as if the mountains came straight down into the sea.

Closer in...closer in. By now the rain was blowing straight into my face, stinging like a whip.

Then came a horrible, crunching groan. The boat had struck a rock. And the next wave rolled it sideways, tipped it up and dumped us in the sea.

4
The empty house

There isn't much you can do when the sea gets hold of you. You try to swim, but you can't be sure which way is up. If you reach the surface, you take a gasping breath. Then the waves roll you over again.

Soon your strength goes. You just want it to end. You're ready to give up and let yourself slide into the depths.

I still don't know how I survived. I just remember finding myself lying on stones, with water swirling past me. A wave must have washed me onto the shore and now the water was rushing back, trying to take me with it.

On hands and knees, I began to crawl over the rocks. It took every bit of my strength. Another wave thundered in, pushing me forward, then dragging me back.

"Jamie! Come on!"

Rob was just in front of me, holding out his hand. He helped me get onto my feet. Fighting against the undertow of the waves, slipping and sliding on the rocks, we finally reached the shore.

At last we were free from the grip of the sea. We were on land, solid land. We both collapsed on the ground and just lay there.

But where was Grandad?

"Your arm's bleeding," said Rob.

I looked at him. "So's your face."

My arm didn't feel painful – or no worse than the rest of me. I was bruised and battered all over. It felt as if all the strength had been washed out of my body.

"Grandad!" I said again.

"I'll go and look for him," Rob said.

He got up painfully. I tried to follow him, but had to sink back down again, completely exhausted.

"Jamie!" Rob had come back. "Don't go to sleep! Not here. We need to find some shelter."

"Did you find Grandad?"

"No."

I realised then that he must be dead. But I tried to push the thought from my mind. If I didn't think about it, maybe it wouldn't be true...

Rob said, "I did see a house, though. Up there – not very far."

He helped me get up. We made our way slowly up the hill, through the lashing rain. But, before long, I could see that the house was empty. Slates had been blown off the roof, and the door had fallen in.

There were no other houses in sight. The house stood alone among a few small fields between the mountainside and the sea. This was the only shelter we were going to find.

It was better than nothing. In the two-roomed house, one room still had a roof over it. There was a fireplace, a stack of dried peat and even a tinderbox, but we couldn't manage to light a fire. We were both shivering in our soaking wet clothes.

Rob opened a door and found a bed built into the wall, with some moth-eaten blankets on it. We wrapped ourselves in the blankets and got into the bed. Still shivering, we lay there, with the wind howling in the chimney and the rain beating against the roof.

"What are we going to do?" I asked. "How will we ever get home?"

"We'll get home all right," Rob said. "Don't you worry. We're on the mainland. When the storm finishes, we'll head for the town and get somebody to take us to the island."

"But we don't know the way."

"Yes we do. We just have to follow the coastline north, and we'll get there all right."

He made it all sound perfectly simple. He was good at doing that – just like Grandad.

Oh, I wished Grandad was there with us. I wished he would walk in right now. I knew exactly what he would say – he'd tell us off for not getting the fire lit. He would do it himself, and the room would fill with light instead of dark shadows. And everything would be all right.

Never again... I was never going to see him again...

I turned my face to the wall. I didn't want Rob to see that I was crying.

The storm lasted for two days and two nights. It was lucky we'd seen the house, because I don't think we would have survived out in the open.

We found a bit of food that the mice hadn't been able to steal – some oatmeal in a heavy-lidded pot. Oatmeal and cold water didn't make the best meal in the world, but we were hungry enough to eat anything.

It was strange that the house had been abandoned, still with some useful things in it. We wondered what had happened to the people who used to live there. A man's jacket hung in a cupboard, all mouldy with damp, alongside a woman's cloak. And there were children's things too.

"Maybe they just got lonely, living in such an out-of-the-way place," I said, "and they decided to move nearer the town."

"So why didn't they take all their things with them? No, something must have happened to them," Rob said.

"Like what?"

"Maybe the wild hunters got them."

I laughed, because it reminded me of what Granny used to say when we were little. "Behave, or else the wild hunters will come and get you, and take you away and eat you!"

"What's funny?" said Rob. "You think they don't exist? My uncle says they do. He's seen them."

"More likely the Norse raiders attacked the place," I said. "It would be an easy target, all alone like this."

"Yes. They stole the sheep, and killed the people."

The thought made me feel nervous. It was getting dark – this was on the second day of our stay. But twilight was the time when raiders tended to strike, landing silently, creeping up from the sea...

"Don't worry," said Rob. "Even the Norsemen won't be out in a storm like this."

All the same, he looked nervous too. He decided to have another go at lighting the fire. For this he needed some kindling – wood shavings or dry straw. The straw we'd tried to light earlier had been useless because it was damp.

I had a sudden idea. I went to look at the mattress on the bed. As I thought, it was just a big sack full of straw, and it felt fairly dry. I untied the sack and pulled out a few handfuls.

Then I felt something odd. Hidden in the straw was something smallish and flat, with hard sides and square corners. It had been carefully hidden... it must be valuable.

What on earth was it?

"Look at this, Rob."

The thing was wrapped up in a bag made of sealskin. I took it out. It was like a small, flat box covered in black leather. But when I lifted the lid, there was nothing much inside. Just a white surface, with strange black marks on it. Actually, lots of white surfaces, thinner than the thinnest cloth.

"It's only a book," said Rob. "Have you never seen one before?"

"No."

"We've got a few of them at home. Here – let me tear out a couple of pages. They make good firelighters."

"Wait a minute," I said. "Why was it hidden away so carefully? Don't burn it. I want to look at it properly."

"Well, you can't do that until we light the fire. It's nearly dark. Pass me some of that straw."

He got the tinderbox and took out the flint and the metal striker. After lots of tries, he made a spark to set light to the straw. The small flame flickered, and we fed it with more straw, then with bits of peat. In the end we had a good fire going.

I put some oats in a pan, to cook porridge. It would make a change from cold oatmeal. Then, in the firelight, we examined the book.

Rob spelled out the name on the front. H-o-l-y. Holly? B-i-b-l-e.

"Holly bibble? What does that mean?" I demanded, but he didn't know.

He flicked through the book, reading bits of it aloud. Often, when he came to a word he didn't know, he had to stop. It was hard to understand what the book was about.

I stared at the black marks, hundreds and hundreds of them, in neat lines through the book. To me they meant nothing at all. But to the book's owner they had held a meaning. Something important – worth keeping, worth hiding.

Carefully I wrapped the book in its sealskin bag.

"What should I do with it?" I asked Rob.

He shrugged. "Keep it, if you want. Finders keepers."

It might be unlucky, I thought. After all, it came from the Old Times. But I wanted to take it. Somehow I felt it would be worth having, and I longed to know its secret.

So, when we left the abandoned house, the book went with me, safe in my pocket.

5
Aftermath

The storm had cleared and it was a bright, sunny morning. Only the sea, still full of rough, grey waves, gave signs that there had ever been a storm.

As we set off along the shore, we looked out for any sign of the boat, or its wreckage. I was half-hoping and half-dreading finding it. If the boat had been washed to shore, then Grandad might still be alive... or we might find his body.

But we saw nothing except the usual things washed up by storms – piles of seaweed, a few bits of driftwood and a plastic bottle or two.

Rob said, "The boat probably sank out there, where it hit the rock."

I was not so sure. I thought it might still be afloat, somewhere out on the ocean. It would run aground on some other shore and pass on its bad luck to the next people who found it.

I hated it, and I hated the sea. Granny was right in saying the sea was our enemy. Maybe it had stopped eating away at the land, but it was still dangerous. It could still eat people up and be hungry for more.

We walked on for ages, following the curve of the coast around the mountain's feet. If we could have gone in a straight line, we could probably have reached the town before nightfall. But the coast didn't run in a straight line. After the mountain, it turned inland, around a long sea loch – a flooded valley stretching far into the hills.

But now we had our first bit of luck. There were a few houses on the shore of the loch, and we called at the first one to ask for some food. When they heard our story, the people were very kind.

"Stay with us the night and I'll take you home in the morning, if the wind's right," said the man of the house.

That evening, as we ate our meal, Rob asked about the abandoned house on the far side of the mountain.

"Do you know who lived there?" he asked.

"A family from the Orkney Isles," said the woman. "They left the isles and settled here because of the Norse raiders."

"They were a bit odd," her husband said.

"What do you mean, odd?" I asked.

He said, "They didn't care what was lucky or unlucky. The woman wore a bright green cloak! That was just asking for trouble. And their daughter never carried a lucky charm to keep her safe."

The woman touched the pocket of her apron, checking that her own bit of luck – some white heather, or maybe a rabbit's foot – was still there. She said, "They believed in a God that looked after them like a father."

"The God of the Old Times," her husband said, and he made the sign people use to turn away bad fortune.

His wife said, "According to them, it all went wrong in the Old Times when people forgot about this God, and got greedy and selfish, and did whatever they liked."

"Maybe they were right," said Rob.

"You think so? I thought it was a load of rubbish, myself," the man said. "And it didn't bring that family any luck."

"What happened to them, then?" I asked.

"We don't know."

"They just disappeared?" Rob said.

"Yes. Maybe the raiders got them in the end. Three or four years ago, it would be, when we found out they were gone."

His wife said, "Maybe they just got tired of living there, and moved on. It was a lonely kind of place to live. I hope they're all right – they were nice enough people."

I wondered what she would say if I showed her the book from the empty house... the book from the Old Times. She would probably think it was unlucky. She would send us away, and sweep out the whole house when we'd gone. So I didn't say a word.

Next day, as he'd promised, the man took us back to the island in his fishing boat. I hurried home. I had been missing for four days and nights, and by now Dad and Granny must think I had been killed in the storm.

I will never forget the look on their faces when they saw me. Dad wrapped me in a huge hug.

"I knew you were all right," my sister said. "I knew you'd come back. But where's Grandad?"

We couldn't even bury him. It was said to be bad luck not to have a body to bury. The proper place was in the kirkyard, where people had been buried right back to the Old Times. Some of the old gravestones were still standing, with the names (so Rob said) of the Ancestors who lay beneath them. The kirk itself – some kind of ancient building – was just a ruin.

Nowadays, no one had the time to spend on carving out gravestones, even if they knew how to write. The dead person would be buried, and sometimes a tree would be planted to mark their grave, or a few stones piled on it.

But we couldn't do that for Grandad. His grave was the sea.

We missed him badly as the year went on. In winter, when the nights were so dreary, he had been the one who cheered us up. He always had a story to tell, or a song to play on his ancient fiddle. Without him, the long nights seemed even longer.

Granny, of course, missed him the most. She was very quiet for a long time. Normally, when she was upset, she would work harder to take her mind off things. But her eyesight was quite bad these days. She couldn't sew or thread up her weaving loom without my sister helping her.

At night, when the wind moaned in the chimney, she would mutter, "It's him. It's him. He's come back to ask why we never gave him a proper burial."

"Granny, it's just the wind," I would tell her, but she didn't seem to hear me. She pulled her cloak around her, shivering.

Dad put some driftwood on the fire, making it blaze and crackle. But still the wind moaned outside, in the darkness of the night.

6
The great ship

Springtime came. By now I was almost 13 years old, tall and strong for my age. Dad trusted me to take the boat out fishing, as long as I didn't go too far from the island. (This was the old boat, slow and clumsy compared to the Ancestors' one, but with better luck. At least I hoped so.)

Rob came with me whenever he could, although his father was getting stricter with him. As a chief's son, Rob had to practise his reading and writing, and learn by heart all the laws of Insh More.

"And it's all such a waste of time," Rob muttered. "I'm never going to be a chief. I want to go adventuring, like Uncle Davie. Are you still going to go to Embra with me, Jamie?"

"Maybe. When we're bigger."

"You keep saying that, but I know what you'll do. You'll get a bit older, marry and settle down, and never leave. Don't you want to see some more of the world? Wouldn't you like something to *really happen* for a change?"

I thought he was asking for trouble when he talked like that. He seemed to have forgotten the last time something *really happened*... when the boat was wrecked and Grandad drowned.

Just then I noticed something strange. It was on the western skyline, like a low, half-hidden cloud. I almost thought it looked like a set of sails on one boat. But no boat ever had as many sails as that, surely? Seven or eight of them, on two – no, it must be three – masts.

Rob saw it too. We both stared and stared.

"It's a ship," Rob said. "At home we've got a picture of a ship like that, from the Old Times."

"Oh, no." At once I changed course, heading for home. I didn't want to have anything to do with another Ancestor boat.

"No, wait, Jamie. I want to see it."

"Well, I don't. It's unlucky."

But before we were anywhere near the shore, the strange ship was much nearer. In spite of myself, I was interested. It was enormous! It must need a dozen people just to keep the sails in trim. And its hull stood higher than a house, with two rows of round windows set into it.

"Have you ever seen anything like it?" breathed Rob.

He knew I hadn't. Nothing like this had been seen off Insh More in my lifetime, or my father's or grandfather's time. And yet it wasn't at all like the Ancestors' boat. It was far bigger, and the hull was built of wood, like a huge version of our fishing boat.

The ship was moving through the water at a good pace, and at first we thought it was heading for the island. But there was nowhere for a ship of that size to moor. Soon it had sailed east of the island, making for the mainland.

"Come on," said Rob. "Follow it. I want to know what it is and where it came from."

"No," I said.

"Jamie, I don't understand you. There I was, grumbling about how nothing ever happens, and when something does come along, you're not interested!"

"We came here to fish," I said. "Start fishing."

By now the ship had disappeared into the mouth of the sea loch where the town lay.

"Well, I'm going to tell everybody about it when we get back," said Rob. "I bet lots of people want to go and look at it."

He was right. The next morning there was a steady stream of boats setting out from the island, heading for the town. Rob went too, with his father and one of his brothers. In the evening he came back, full of excitement.

"The ship came all the way from Embra!" he told us. "It's called the *Castle*. It belongs to the King of Lothian, and he sent it out to sail up the west coast, exploring, making new maps."

"What's exploring?" my sister asked. "What are maps?"

Rob said, "A map is like a picture of the land and sea, the way an eagle would see it from up in the sky."

"Whatever for?" she wanted to know.

Rob ignored her. He was still full of news. "And they have some very clever people on board. There's a... What's he called again? A docker, or something. He can make sick people better."

"How?" I demanded.

"Well, the smith's wife was having a baby. It was a difficult birth – she'd been having birth pains for days. This docker... no, doctor... put her to sleep somehow, cut her open, took out the baby and sewed her up again!"

"I don't like the sound of that," said Granny. "It sounds like witchcraft or evil knowledge from the Old Times."

"Is she still alive, the smith's wife?" I asked.

"Yes, she's fine, and so is the baby. Oh, and another thing they can do – make people see better. They gave my father two little bits of thin, see-through stuff, held together with metal. He put them in front of his eyes and he said he could see things so clearly, it was like being a boy again."

"Maybe we could get some for you," Dad said to Granny.

She looked doubtful. "But if they're using knowledge from the Old Times... "

"Not everything was bad in the Old Times," Rob said. "Not everything was unlucky. There was a lot of useful knowledge that's been forgotten. And that's the other reason the ship is here... to buy books. Books that have got knowledge in them. The king wants to collect all the books that are left, before they get too old to be readable."

Before Elspeth could start asking what books were, I said, "Is your father going to sell some of the books from your house?"

"Maybe. He's going to take a few of them tomorrow, to show the king's men. We've got at least 20 books at home. Father says there used to be hundreds of the things."

"Hundreds?" I said, disbelieving. "What happened to them all?"

"Half of them got ruined when the roof leaked. And people used the rest for lighting fires or tore out the pages to write on."

I asked him how much they were worth, because I had just remembered that I had a book of my own. Rob knew about it, of course, but no one else did. For months it had been hidden away in the smokehouse roof, where it had stayed quite safe and dry, although it had begun to smell of smoked haddock.

Rob said, "They're paying in copper or iron for every book they get. Enough iron to make a sword, Jamie! Wouldn't you like to have a sword of your own?"

Of course I would. At once I decided I would sell the book, which was no use to me since I couldn't read it. A sword would be far more useful. Or a new blade for our rusty old plough.

I went to fetch the book, but Granny – as soon as she realised what it was – got upset.

"Are you crazy? Haven't the Old Times brought us enough bad luck? I'm not having that thing in the house!"

She snatched the book out of my hand, went to the door and threw it out. I heard it land with a dull thud somewhere in the field outside.

There was no point arguing with her. When people think a thing is unlucky, it's very hard to change their minds. Later, though, I rescued the book, wrapped it up again and hid it away.

Tomorrow, somehow, I would have to find a way of getting it to the town.

7
Ali

The next day, and the day after that, the wind died away to nothing. I couldn't row all the way to the town – it would have taken hours. Anyway, Dad needed me to help with the sheep-shearing.

By the third day we had finished the sheep, and a breeze was blowing. I asked Dad if I could go out fishing. Just as I was getting the boat ready, Rob arrived.

"Are you going to the town? Are you taking that book?"

"Yes. Want to come with me?"

It was a daft question. Of course he wanted to go.

He said, "Father's taking some books over, but all my brothers want to go too, and there's no room for me. It's not fair! Just because I'm the youngest, they never let me do anything!" This was something he was always getting annoyed about.

"Come on, Rob. Give me a hand to get the boat in the water."

Three or four other boats were ahead of us, sailing towards the town. I was pretty sure most people didn't have books to sell, like I did. Maybe they wanted to see the doctor. Or maybe they were just curious.

We sailed into the sheltered sea loch where the town lay. I know now that it wasn't a very big town, but in those days it seemed big to me – about 30 houses, all clustered together, not scattered among fields. It had a quay where boats could be tied up.

Something was happening there. I saw a crowd of people on the quayside, near the great ship. They were shouting – the sound carried across the water. And on the ship itself there was a lot of activity. The sails were being unfurled.

"We're too late," Rob groaned. "The ship's leaving."

Slowly, the ship slid away from the quay. But what were the people on shore doing? Not waving goodbye – that was for sure. They seemed to be throwing things at the ship. Stones, probably. I saw a few arrows being fired as well.

The ship's sails filled. The gap widened between ship and shore. Then came a loud noise, louder than anything I'd ever heard before... louder than thunder overhead. It echoed against the hills.

A puff of smoke billowed out from the side of the ship. That terrifying noise came again, and people screamed.

At the end of the quay, there was a stone pillar with a sort of metal basket on top. The townspeople used to light a fire there at night, to guide boats safely in. Now it was gone – pillar, basket and everything.

"What happened?" I gasped. But Rob didn't know.

Again that sound. This time, a hole appeared in the harbour wall, round and dark like the centre of an eye. By now the people on shore were running in all directions. No one was attacking the ship any more and soon it was well beyond the range of their arrows.

The ship sailed past us slowly, making for the mouth of the loch. We gazed after it, fascinated and scared.

"However do they do that?" asked Rob. "Knocking holes in things, like a giant throwing rocks."

"Granny would say it was evil knowledge from the Old Times," I said. "She'd say they were bringers of bad luck, the whole shipload of them."

"But they didn't actually kill anyone," Rob said.

I looked back at the town. I could see the other boats from Insh More arriving at the quay. Now that the ship was well out of reach, the crowd had gathered again, shouting and waving swords.

Suddenly, a movement caught my eye. Someone was running along the shore, away from the town and towards the mouth of the loch. It looked as if he was chasing after the ship.

I pointed him out to Rob.

"He must be from the ship," said Rob. "They all wear that colour of blue. He's got left behind."

"He'll never catch up," I said, for by now the ship was about to round the point where the loch met the open sea.

"Hey there!" The running figure had come to a stop. He was waving desperately. "Come here! Take me out to the *Castle*, and I'll make sure you get well paid for it!"

Was he talking to us? He must be. Our boat was the only one out on the water.

Cautiously we sailed closer in. The sailor waded into the water, coming to meet us. He didn't look much older than us, although he wore the uniform of the king's ship. He had short, fair hair and a thin, girlish-looking face.

Now he was up to his waist in the water, and he clearly didn't want to go any deeper. "Come on! Hurry up!" he ordered us.

We looked at each other. Why should we help him? He wasn't one of our people. In fact, his ship seemed to have attacked the town, or maybe the town had attacked the ship – so we were his enemies.

Still, I felt sorry for him, especially when he stopped trying to order us around. "Please," he begged. "You're my only hope. If that lot catch me, they'll kill me!" And he looked back over his shoulder, towards the town.

Suddenly I made up my mind. We took the boat in closer and, between us, we managed to pull him into the boat. It rocked dangerously, then steadied.

We set out after the great sailing ship. At first we seemed to gain on it. But then, as it got out onto the open sea, we couldn't match its speed. Further ahead it sailed, with the sun shining white on its sails.

"It's no use," said Rob. "We can never catch them. Not unless they turn and come back for you."

"They won't do that." The boy's voice was flat and hopeless. "I'm just a cabin hand. They won't even miss me until they need me to serve up the captain's meal."

"How did you get left behind?" I asked.

"It wasn't my fault! I went ashore to have a look around and suddenly there was this crowd of people all around me, yelling. I couldn't even hear what half of them were saying. Somebody had gone to the ship's doctor and taken some medicine, and the next day he was dead – something like that. They said we'd brought bad luck with us. And then they started attacking the ship, and forgot about me. So I ran away."

Rob leaned forward. "When the ship was under attack – what happened? You know, that loud noise?"

"The cannons," the boy said, grinning. "They fire balls of iron as big as your head. Not bad weapons, are they? We knew we might need them to fight off the Norse raiders. We never thought we'd have to turn them against our own people."

"What do you mean – your own people?" I said. "This isn't the land of Lothian. We don't obey your king."

"We have our own chiefs to lead us," said Rob. "In fact, my father is a chief. And we don't like outsiders telling us what to do."

"Yes, I noticed that," the boy said.

"What are you going to do now?" I asked him.

"I don't know. I'll have to try and make my own way home somehow." And he looked longingly after the ship, which was far away by now, beyond the island.

"Back to Embra? It's a long way," I said.

"Look, I'm not stupid! I've done that journey and you haven't. You're just... " And then he stopped.

I could guess what he'd been about to say. *You're just dumb country boys that have never been anywhere or seen anything.* But then he looked around and realised that he was alone with us, in our boat, a long way out from land. He'd better be polite to us.

Rob had been watching him closely. He suddenly asked, "What's your name?"

"Ali."

"Short for...?"

I expected the answer to be Alistair. But it was "Alison".

"Alison?" I said, disbelieving. "Around here, that's a girl's name. Why did they give you a girl's name?"

"Because I'm a girl." A huge grin spread across Ali's face. "Are you really telling me you didn't know?"

8
The plan

I was completely lost for words. A girl! A girl with short hair, wearing trousers! A girl who worked on a ship! That was the worst thing. Everyone knew it was bad luck to have females on a boat.

I looked uneasily at Rob. Although he seemed to have guessed the truth before I did, he still looked quite shocked.

"Are there many women on board the *Castle*?" he asked the girl.

"Not that many. Seven of us."

"But it's very unlucky," I said. Already, I was heading for shore. I wanted to get her out of my boat as soon as possible.

"What do you mean, unlucky?" she asked.

"I mean what I say. It's unlucky to be on a boat if there are women on it."

"That's the daftest thing I ever heard. And what about the women that live on islands? How are they supposed to leave the place - by swimming?"

"They don't leave. Why would they want to?"

Now it was Ali's turn to look shocked. "So, if you're a girl, born on an island like that one over there, you can never leave it? You're a prisoner?"

I hadn't thought of it like that. I was used to things as they were – the men and boys went fishing, the women stayed at home. But it was true that my sister had never been off the island, not even as far as the town. Did she feel like a prisoner? I'd have to ask her.

Ali said, "If women aren't allowed on boats, how do you know it's bad luck?"

"It just is. Everybody knows that."

"No, they don't. They don't think like that where I come from. It's a daft idea!"

We had reached the island. The boat's hull crunched into the shingle.

"There, see?" she said. "Your boat didn't sink, even though I was on it."

"Get out," I told her. I didn't really feel safe until we had pulled the boat well up onto the shore.

Ali scrambled up onto a rock and looked out to sea. The *Castle* had vanished beyond the horizon. Then she looked around at the island, with its stone-walled fields and bare, treeless hills. She didn't seem to think much of it.

"Do you actually live here?" she asked. "I would die of boredom!"

Rob said, "What are you going to do now?"

"I don't know." She suddenly looked lost and lonely. For a moment I almost felt sorry for her. Then she said, "I know one thing, though. I'm not going to spend the rest of my life as a prisoner on this island!"

"You'd better come back to my house," said Rob. "My father will decide what's the best thing to do."

But even the chief couldn't solve the problem of Ali.

The best thing would be to find some way of getting her back to the ship. The problem was that no one knew where the ship was making for. There were lots of islands to the north and west, waiting to be explored. The *Castle* could have sailed to any of a dozen different places.

Or Ali could try to get back to Embra, either by land or sea. It would be a difficult journey for a girl on her own. She had never learned to sail a small boat, and in any case, no one had a boat to give away to a stranger. As for travelling overland, that was dangerous. It would be easy to get lost in the high mountains or captured by the wild hunters.

Two days later, Ali was still at Rob's house. He brought her to see me, down on the shore. I was mending a net, with my sister helping, but Rob persuaded Elspeth to go back home. He didn't want her to hear what he was going to say.

"We've got a plan," he said. "Do you want to be in on it?"

"Depends what it is."

"You have to promise not to tell anybody."

I promised, already pretty sure I knew what the plan was.

"Let me guess – you're going to Embra," I said. "But where will you get a boat?"

"I thought we could maybe use your one. You could come too," he said hastily.

"You can't have our boat. We need it for fishing."

"But I'd bring it back right away. I could be there and back in a month."

"A month! If we lose a month's fishing now, we won't be able to live through the winter!" (It was midsummer, but the thought of winter was always there at the back of my mind.)

Rob looked disappointed. He thought for a moment.

"There is another boat we could take," he said. "Uncle Davie's one. He never uses it nowadays."

Rob's uncle – the one who had gone off to Embra years ago – lived a quiet life these days. He'd fallen down and broken his leg, which had never mended properly. He stayed at home now and spent his time making whisky. People said he drank most of it himself.

"Would he let you have his boat?" I asked.

"I wouldn't ask him; I'd just take it. Otherwise he'd want to come with us. And that would be a disaster."

Ali spoke for the first time. "What's the boat like? Is it any bigger than that one?" She pointed to our boat.

"Not really."

"But it's tiny! We'll never get home in a boat like that!"

"Uncle Davie got to Embra and back all right," said Rob. "It's not like a ship. We wouldn't live on board. We'd just sail during the day and find someplace to land at night, or in bad weather."

Ali looked extremely doubtful.

I saw that she was still wearing her blue uniform jacket, but not her trousers. Instead, she had a grey tweed skirt like the ones the island women wore. It was a weird mixture. She saw me looking at her and got angry.

"They took my clothes away – to dry them off, they said – and wouldn't give me my trousers back. They said it's unlucky for girls to wear trousers. I've never heard such a load of rubbish!"

"Is it rubbish, though? You didn't seem to be having much luck when you got abandoned," I reminded her.

"That wasn't because of bad luck. It's because of the brainless idiots that attacked the ship. Our gunners should have blasted them out of existence!"

The girl had quite a temper. I wondered how she and Rob would get on together, if they really set off for

Embra. They'd probably hate each other long before they got there.

Rob began trying to persuade me to go with them. I could see why – he wanted someone on his side if an argument started.

I told him I couldn't leave Dad to cope with the harvest on his own. He would need my help. When oats are ripe, you have to harvest them as soon as you can, before the next storm flattens them.

"The oats are still green. They won't be ready for ages yet," said Rob. "What if I promised we would be back here before harvest? Would you come with us then?"

"Dad would never let me do it. He'd be afraid I would drown myself, like Grandad."

"You don't have to tell him," Ali said. "We're going to leave early one morning, before anyone's up. We'll be miles away and they won't even know we're gone."

Suddenly I could picture them in my mind, setting out at first light. The wind of morning would fill the sail. Before the day's end, the boat would round the headland far to the south and go on to the unknown lands beyond.

And I would be left here, wishing that I had gone too.

"Come with us, Jamie," said Rob. "I know you want to."

I said nothing.

He thought of another way to persuade me. "Don't forget that book of yours. You could take it to Embra – I bet it's worth a lot of metal. Your dad needs a new plough blade, doesn't he? You could bring back enough iron to make one. And then he wouldn't be angry with you for going. He'd say you were right to do it."

That was what made my mind up.

"All right," I said. "I'll go."

9
Anything that moves

Rob, always restless, wanted to set sail the very next day. But I refused to go without testing out his uncle's boat. "Never trust strangers, dogs or boats until you get to know them," as Grandad used to say.

The boat was fine, apart from one edge of the sail that needed to be re-stitched. Back ashore, I did the work while the other two discussed what we should take with us. Food and water, obviously. My bow, Rob's dagger, and some fishing gear. A tinderbox and a pan, so that we could cook what we caught. Rob had a bit of money saved up and I had my book. Ali, of course, had nothing.

I still felt uneasy about taking a girl on board a boat. It might not mean bad luck to Embra people – but this wasn't Embra. All day I looked out for omens about our journey. Wild geese flying seawards... a good omen. Rob tripping over a mooring rope... bad. A dead fish that got washed up near my feet... bad, very bad.

The other thing that troubled me was my family. What would they think when they found I had disappeared? For the first time in my life, I wished I could write and they could read. Then I could leave them a message.

"I'll write a letter to my father," Rob said. "He'll tell your family where you've gone."

"Okay. Make sure to write that I'll be back before harvest time."

"You can write?" Ali gave him a disbelieving look.

"Of course. Can't you?"

"No."

Rob looked pleased. He'd found something he knew more about than Ali did.

Using a piece of charcoal and a blank end-page torn out of my book, he wrote some words to explain our plans. He would leave the message on his bed, to be found after we had gone.

Now we were ready and the weather looked good. There was no reason to wait any longer.

"We'll go tomorrow," said Rob.

As the boat slipped away from Insh More, I couldn't help looking back. It was all very well making promises to be home soon, but what if something happened? Another bad storm, another shipwreck, and I might never see my home and family again. And I hadn't even said goodbye.

I don't believe Rob looked back once. He was too busy thinking about what lay ahead, and asking Ali about her voyage on the *Castle*.

"How did you decide to become a sailor?" he asked.

"I suppose I was bored with life at home. My mum and dad have a clothes shop, and my sisters are quite happy working there, telling rich old ladies how nice they look." She scowled at the thought. "I hated it. I wanted to get out and do something different."

It was funny. Rob was bored at home, so he wanted to go to Embra. Ali had done the opposite journey, for the same reason.

"If we go back the way you came, we should get to Embra all right," Rob said.

"Yes, but it wouldn't be the quickest way to get there. We were sailing all around the islands, exploring. And anyway, I don't know if I can remember where we went. All these hills and lochs and islands look the same to me."

Ali had somehow managed to get her uniform trousers back. She was looking like a sailor again, instead of an island woman. But she wasn't acting much like a sailor. In fact, as the wind got up and the waves started getting choppy, she looked quite seasick.

"What's the matter? This is just a gentle breeze," I said. "You must have sailed through heavier seas than this on the *Castle*."

"The *Castle* didn't roll about like this toy boat of yours." She was holding onto the side of the boat, as if she was scared of being tipped out. "What are you laughing at? It isn't funny! I feel terrible!"

"Do you want to go back?" Rob asked.

She swallowed hard. "No. Carry on."

With this wind, we were making good speed. I looked back again, wondering if anyone had noticed our absence yet. Would they try to come after us and stop us? They would never catch up with us now. We had too good a start.

In mid-afternoon we passed the southern headland. The only time I had been here before was with Grandad, the day before the storm. We didn't stop, but sailed on southwards, making the best of the wind. On our left was the mainland, with mountains I'd never seen before. On our right were a few islands, and beyond them the open sea.

"I wonder where you would get to," Rob said, "if you sailed out past the islands and kept on going. Does the sea go on forever?"

I could see Ali thought this was a dumb question. "You'd get to a land called America. Have you never heard of it?"

"No."

She said, "In Embra there are maps from the Old Times, showing the whole world. You'd be amazed – Scotland is just a tiny part of it. There are lots of other countries and some of them are huge. Or they were, before the sea rose."

"So the maps aren't accurate any more," I said. "How do you know this America place still exists? Has anyone ever been there?"

"Not since the Old Times. But the king's planning to send out an expedition in a few years. The ships are being built right now."

Rob looked interested. He asked lots of questions, but Ali couldn't answer most of them. He sighed.

"I'd love to sail far out to the west and explore new places."

"First we'd better explore someplace to spend the night," I said, for the sun was going down.

There were no houses along this stretch of coast. The mountains came down steeply to the sea with pine forests along their slopes. We found a small bay, which had a pebble beach and a stream to give us water. I had caught a few fish to cook for our supper, so we gathered firewood and piled it on the shore.

But, before we lit our fire, Rob led us up the hill so that we could see what our next day's journey would be like.

From above the treeline we had an amazing view. There was a glorious sunset beyond the western isles. To the north, Insh More lay on the far horizon. To the southwest the mainland hills stretched out into a long peninsula. Or could it be an island?

Rob frowned. "I wonder if we have to go right around that point. Ali, do you know if there's a gap we can sail through?"

"I told you, all these hills and islands look the same to me," she said.

"We should get back to the boat," I said uneasily. "It'll be dark soon."

"Scared of the dark, are you?" Ali said, grinning.

"Not of the dark – no. But there might be wild dogs in this forest." As I said it I was stringing my bow. It was best to be ready.

"Dogs! He's scared of dogs!"

"Shut up!" said Rob. "I bet you've never met a pack of wild dogs, have you?"

"No. But surely they don't hunt people?"

"They hunt anything. Anything that moves."

We went back down through the forest, where the shadows were getting thicker and darker every moment. I couldn't help looking around anxiously. But we got safely back to the beach.

We lit the fire, and fed it with branches. Then I speared the fish on long sticks and put them to roast over the flames. They smelled wonderful.

We were not the only ones who liked the smell of them. When I looked up from the fire, I saw some eyes staring back from the darkness. The firelight glittered in the depths of them.

Five... seven... a dozen pairs of eyes, in a half-circle between us and the trees. They were low down. Animal eyes, not human.

Afraid to speak, I grabbed Rob's arm and pointed. He jumped as if I'd bitten him.

Now we could see them in the firelight. They were dogs all right, but bigger – much bigger – than our sheepdog. Their teeth looked sharp enough to rip out the throat of a deer. Or a man.

And they were creeping closer. When one stayed still, another moved. They were closing in on us. Soon we would be surrounded.

They didn't like the fire. You could see them flinch when it blazed up and spat out sparks. If only we had gathered more firewood! There was hardly any left now, and the dogs were between us and the forest.

"Don't look so scared," Ali said. "They're just dogs. Man's best friend."

"These are *wild* dogs – man's worst enemy," I said. "They could kill you."

She smiled that infuriating smile. I could see she didn't believe a word I said.

But soon the dogs would prove to her that I was right.

10
Man's worst enemy

We couldn't get away on foot. Dogs can run much faster than people. There was only one way to escape – in the boat. It was just a few paces behind us, pulled up on the shore.

"Come on," I said to Rob. "Help me to launch the boat."

Slowly, so as not to excite the dogs, we slid the boat into the water. The dogs watched us. Any moment, I expected them to rush at us... but maybe they were more interested in the fish.

"Get in the boat," I told Ali.

"What? Without my supper? No way!"

I couldn't believe what she did next. She darted towards the fire, snatched up a stick with a fish on it, and started to run back. She had a triumphant smile on her face.

Instantly the dogs were after her. The biggest one jumped up, trying to grab the stick that she was waving like a spear. His huge jaws took hold of her arm and he pulled her to the ground.

She wasn't smiling now. She was screaming in pain. What could we do? We couldn't just leave her there! They would eat her alive!

I put an arrow on the string, aimed and fired, all in a moment. At that range I couldn't miss. The big dog howled and let go of Ali. But the others were all around her, snarling and growling.

Rob snatched up a spare oar from the boat and started hitting out at the nearest dogs. They leapt away from him, but then they came back. He was surrounded by angry dogs. I had an arrow ready, waiting for the moment when one of them got him.

He made it as far as the fire. There he picked up a branch that was well alight at one end. He swung it around him and the dogs jumped back. They were more scared of fire than of arrows or clubs.

Using the burning branch to keep the dogs back, he got to Ali and helped her up. She staggered down to the water's edge and managed to climb into the boat. When we were all on-board, I rowed out to deeper water and dropped the anchor stone.

The dogs didn't try to swim after us. They were fighting over the fish by now, and howling because it was hot enough to burn their mouths.

"Are you all right?" Rob asked Ali.

She moaned. By the light of the burning branch, I could see that her sleeve was soaked in blood.

Rob made her take her jacket off so that we could look at the wound. The dog's teeth had gone right into her arm and blood was still pouring out.

"Tie something around my arm," she gasped. "A bit of rope – anything. No, here, look – higher up."

It was the right thing to do. Soon the bleeding seemed to stop. But her face was very pale – she must have lost a lot of blood.

She lay down in the bottom of the boat and slept, or maybe fainted, for a while. The branch burned down, and I dropped it in the water. On shore, the dying light of our fire showed the dogs still prowling around.

"You get some sleep," I said to Rob. "I'll keep watch."

The bottom of a boat isn't the best place to sleep, but he managed to do it. I stayed awake through the rest of the short summer night.

I was wondering why on earth I'd agreed to come on this journey. To help Ali? She was an idiot who wouldn't listen to other people. She would probably get herself killed, and us too. Was it because I wanted adventure? This night had shown me enough adventure to last for a long time.

Maybe we should go home. We were too young to be going on a journey like this. It was far too dangerous.

But I knew Rob would never agree to turn back. He was braver than me. Also, he hated to admit defeat...

and it would be a defeat. We had hardly even started on our journey – he would never go back at this stage.

A small breeze came with the rising sun. I wakened Rob, leaving Ali asleep. We pulled up the anchor and set out, sailing south and west along the mainland coast. It was all forest and mountains until we came to a wide inlet of the sea. Was it just a sea loch, leading into the mountains? Or was the land on one side of it really an island?

We could tell by the sun that the inlet led eastwards, which was more the way we wanted to go. Also, there were a few fields and houses along the edge of it. Maybe someone would give us food.

Ali began to wake up. She looked terrible. When she tried to move, she moaned in pain. Her hand and arm had swollen up like a bloated, rotting fish.

"Should we untie that rope that was stopping the bleeding?" Rob asked her.

"Is it still there? You shouldn't have left it on for as long as this!" she said angrily.

"Well, how was I to know?"

He undid the rope. I half-expected the bleeding to start again, but nothing seemed to happen. Her arm was still swollen, though. She could hardly bend it. She couldn't put her jacket on again and she was shivering.

"We need help," Rob said, and he steered the boat towards a landing-place near a house.

The woman of the house didn't like the look of us, especially when she heard about the dog bite. She didn't let us in. But she did give us some hot porridge, which we had to eat standing outside.

"What's she so scared of?" Ali muttered.

"You," I said. "It's very unlucky to get bitten by a wild dog. You might go mad and start biting other people. Then you die, and so do they. There's no cure."

"Oh, thanks. That's really cheered me up."

"It's your own stupid fault," I said. "You'd never have got bitten if you'd got in the boat when I said."

"Stop it," said Rob. "It's happened. There's no use arguing about it now, is there?"

He knocked on the door and talked to the woman again. Being Rob, he managed to persuade her to give him some bits of cloth to bandage Ali's arm and keep the flies off. He also bought a cloak for her to wear. And he got some useful information.

"I was right – this is an island," he told us. "We don't have to sail a long way westwards. We can carry on eastwards through the gap between the island and the mainland. Ali, do you feel well enough to go on?"

Ali nodded.

We thanked the woman and said goodbye. She said, "Fortune go with you! And remember what I said about the Straits of Ness."

Walking back to the boat, I asked Rob what the woman had meant.

"She said to keep away from the Straits of Ness because there are monsters there... huge great sea creatures that can swallow people whole. I don't believe her, though. I think she was just trying to scare me."

"Let's hope so," I said. "But hurry up! This wind isn't going to last all day!"

11

The shepherd boy

I was right about the wind. By the middle of the day it had died down completely and we had to start rowing. Ali, of course, couldn't help with this. She sat still, looking deathly pale, her cloak wrapped tightly around her.

The loch had got narrower, winding between the hills. Each time I looked ahead, I expected to see it opening out again, leading to the sea. But it narrowed more, and the hills got higher and steeper. There were no houses here. This sort of land was no good for anything except deer-hunting.

I began to wonder where we would spend the night. We might have to sleep on the bare mountainside, without even wood to make a fire. And what if there were more wild dogs around?

We could try to sleep in the boat. But even here, so far from the open sea, the water was restless. I didn't think I would sleep too well.

The mountains were all around us now. They seemed empty of life. Nothing moved, except for an eagle circling high above us and the shifting shadows of clouds.

Then I saw some sheep on the mountainside. Where there were sheep, there must be people. And soon, coming around a curve of the valley, we saw more sheep. A man and a young boy had started gathering them in for the night. There was a sheep pen and a shepherd's hut beside it.

The shepherd was quite friendly, although his boy didn't say a word. He just stared at us. I guessed he didn't see many strangers.

"Of course you can stay the night with us," the shepherd said. "Donnie was just about to go hunting. If luck's with him, there'll be enough food for all of us."

"I could go too, if you like," I said to the boy.

Donnie didn't react at all. Didn't he want me to go? Then his father started making mysterious signs to him and pointing at me. I realised the boy was deaf and speechless.

He was a good archer, though. We hadn't been out for very long before he shot a mountain hare. I saw another one and had a go at it, but missed. Donnie gave me a pitying look.

A peat fire was burning when we got back, with a pot of potatoes on it. While we waited for the meat to cook, the shepherd hardly stopped talking. He wanted to know all about us.

He had a look at Ali's arm and said she should eat the hair of a dog – that would help to heal the wound. He gave her a hair from one of his sheepdogs. But she couldn't eat it, or anything else. Instead of looking pale, she was now flushed and feverish. She said even the smell of food made her feel sick.

That was fine with me. All the more food for the rest of us.

I slept well that night on a bed of dry heather. Even the bleating of the sheep couldn't keep me awake. When I woke, I was keen to carry on with our journey, but I soon saw it would be impossible. Ali was very ill.

She lay restlessly, tossing and turning. Her face was still flushed. Her eyes were open but she didn't seem to know where she was and, when we spoke to her, she didn't answer.

"Has she got that mad dog sickness?" I asked Rob, but he didn't know. We'd heard of the sickness, but had never seen anyone who actually had it.

I didn't want to go near her. Rob was braver than me.

"She needs water to cool down the fever," he said, and he brought her drink after drink from the nearby stream. Sometimes she managed to swallow a bit; other times she just knocked the cup away and spilt it.

I didn't want to be there if Ali suddenly went crazy and started biting people. I decided to go fishing. We couldn't keep on eating the shepherd's food without giving him something in return.

I came back in the late afternoon. Rob was sitting on a rock, reading my book, which I'd left in the hut.

"Sorry," he said, putting the book down and looking guilty. "I didn't think you'd mind if I had a look at it. I can read much better now than when you first found it."

"I don't mind," I said, although actually I did feel a bit resentful. It was my book, even if I couldn't understand a single page. "Read me a bit, while I clean the fish. How's Ali, by the way?"

"Oh... I nearly forgot about her. I'll just go and see."

When he came out, he said, "She's still the same. Burning up with fever."

"She'll die, won't she, if she goes on like this?"

He didn't answer. His face was anxious and I realised that he didn't want her to die. As for me, I didn't care either way. I didn't like Ali – I thought she was an idiot. And I could tell she felt the same about me.

Rob picked up my book again, as if he wanted to take his mind off the problem of Ali. He started reading aloud to me. It was a story about a shepherd who had a hundred sheep but one got lost. The shepherd went out looking for it and didn't stop until he had found it.

Then he read another story, and another. I liked hearing them. The tales Granny told on winter nights were so familiar that I was bored with them, but these were all new to me.

After we had eaten that night, Rob offered to read some more. The shepherd liked the stories too. His boy, of course, couldn't hear them. He sat whittling away with a knife, carving something out of wood.

"Who's this Jesus that the stories are all about?" the shepherd asked.

I was wondering the same thing myself. I had heard the word before, but not as the name of a person. It was just something people said if they were shocked or angry.

"I don't know who he was," Rob said. "There's a lot more that I haven't read yet. Do you want me to carry on?"

Rob read about how Jesus made sick people well and even brought a dead girl to life again. As he read it, he glanced towards the hut, and I guessed what he was thinking. If only this Jesus was here now, he'd make Ali better in an instant. He could probably make Donnie hear and speak as well.

"Are these stories true?" the shepherd asked. "Did they really happen?"

"Of course they did, or why would they be written in a book?" I said.

Rob laughed. "Not everything in books really happened, you know, Jamie. There are made-up stories in books. We've got one at home about a talking cat. And another one about men going to the moon."

I didn't like it when he laughed at me. It wasn't my fault that he knew more than I did. If I'd been born the son of a chief, I would be able to read just as well as Rob. Maybe better.

"Read another bit," the shepherd said.

But now the light was fading and Rob's eyes were getting tired. He closed the book and put it away carefully in its bag.

Donnie was still whittling at his piece of wood. He'd made something that looked quite like a snake – long and straight, with a pointed end. But the head was wrong. It was more like a fierce dog's head, held upright on a narrow neck.

"What's he making?" I asked the shepherd.

"I think it's the monster of Ness. He saw it a few weeks ago."

"He saw a monster!" Rob was excited. "And it didn't kill him?"

"Maybe it didn't see him. It was early one morning, very misty. I was attending to a sick sheep and I didn't see anything myself. All I know is, Donnie saw *something* down at the loch. He came running back here, and he was scared to death. This is the only way he can show me what he saw."

He passed the little carving over so that we could look at it.

"How big was this thing?" I asked. The shepherd asked Donnie the same question with signs, pointing at the carving, then stretching his hands out wide.

Donnie got up and started walking. He walked for twenty... thirty... almost forty paces. Then he turned and stood still, looking at us.

"Scary," I said. "I hope we don't meet this creature."

"What are these lines he's carved on the sides?" Rob asked.

"I don't know," the shepherd said. He tried to ask Donnie about them. But all the answer he got was Donnie moving his arms as if he was rowing a boat – rowing fast, heaving the boat through the water.

That was easy to understand. If you see the monster, get away as fast as you can.

"Don't worry. We will," said Rob.

"If we can," I added under my breath.

12
Head of a dog

The next day, Ali was no better. She lay with her eyes shut, talking to herself in a meaningless babble, as if she was trapped inside a horrible dream. Rob tried to wake her, but his voice didn't seem to get through. He couldn't even get her to drink anything now.

"If only my wife was here," the shepherd said. "She'd know what to do."

I was surprised to hear that he had a wife. He told us that his real home was further east, along the valley. His wife and four other children lived there all the time. For a few months each year he brought the sheep out here for the summer grazing.

"Did you think I would live in this hut all through the winter?" he said. "Not me. It's lonely enough in summer, with just Donnie for company. But in the winter, when the wild dogs get hungry... " He shivered at the thought.

"Maybe we could take Ali to your wife," Rob suggested.

"Don't be daft," I said. "She's too sick. She'd probably try to throw herself in the water and capsize the boat."

"Moira will be here in a day or two," the shepherd said. "She brings us some food supplies every now and then. But I don't know if... "

He stopped talking, but I could guess what he'd been going to say – Ali might not survive until then.

Rob walked away. He went down to the lochside and stared out across the water. He seemed to be talking to himself. Oh, no... had he caught Ali's disease? He should have kept well away from her like I had.

Not long after, Donnie got excited. He was pointing eastwards, to where a rowing boat had come around the curve of the valley. As it got nearer, I saw that a woman was rowing it with long, steady strokes. She had a young girl with her.

"It's Moira," the shepherd said, surprised. "She's got here sooner than I thought."

When Moira heard about Ali, she came hurrying up the hill. She took charge straight away. Getting Rob to fetch some water from the stream, she put a cool, damp cloth on Ali's hot forehead. Then she unwrapped the bandage on her arm. The wound looked very bad, smelly and swollen, with yellow stuff coming out of it.

"A hot poultice – that's what this needs," she said.

She sent her daughter out to gather herbs and dock leaves. Meanwhile she boiled up a pan of water over the fire. All the time she talked soothingly to Ali, as if she was a little child.

The hot poultice was a pad of clean wool, boiled up with dock leaves and placed over the wound. Moira tied it in place with strips of cloth from the edge of Ali's cloak. The old, stinking bandages went into the fire.

"Keep on washing her face with cold water," Moira told Rob. "It will help to bring the fever down."

Even before the sun began to sink, Ali started looking better. She was cooler and her feverish mumblings had quietened. She drank some water too. Nobody said, "She's going to be all right" – that would only bring bad luck. But everyone was thinking it.

"Keep on with the hot poultices until the swelling has gone down," Moira told us. "And get her to drink as much as you can. If she takes a turn for the worse again, come and get me. But now I have to get back to my young ones before dark."

Rob said, "Can I ask you something? Why did you decide to come here today?"

"Now, that's a funny thing. I was going to leave in a day or two, when I'd had time to do some baking. But I just had a feeling something wasn't quite right. It was like a voice was telling me, 'Go. Go today'."

Rob smiled, as if her answer pleased him.

"Do you know why Moira came here today?" he said to me, after she had gone. "It's because I did what it says in that book of yours. I prayed to God and asked for help. And God answered me."

I thought this was weird.

"Does it really say that in the book?"

"Yes. It says, 'Ask and it will be given to you'."

"OK then," I said, sarcastically. "Why don't you ask for a few more things? Like some fish for supper. I won't bother to try and catch any. You just ask for some and see if God sends them. Maybe they'll jump right out of the water into our hands."

"Laugh as much as you like," said Rob. "All I know is, I prayed for help and I got it."

And he walked off, leaving me standing there.

We stayed with the shepherd for several more days, while Ali got better. Rob spent most of the time reading my book. He read us some other stories. I remember a good one about a long-ago flood that had covered the whole earth.

"But God promised there would never be such a bad flood again," Rob said. "And he has kept his promise."

"Yeah – so far," I said.

I couldn't understand why the book fascinated him so much. He tried to explain.

"It says that God, who made the whole earth, loves every one of us. He loves us like a father. But people didn't obey him and everything went wrong. That's why he sent Jesus to live on earth... "

There was a lot more of this. I got bored with listening and went fishing again.

A few days later Ali was much better – no more fever and her wound was healing well. We said goodbye to the shepherd and his boy. It was time to go on with our journey.

With a light breeze behind us, we sailed eastwards along the narrow valley. After a time it broadened out. There were a few houses standing among fields, and Moira's daughter waved at us from a doorway.

Then came another narrow valley, with dark, frowning pine forests on either side. We heard a dog barking far away and Ali looked around nervously. I thought this was a good thing. She had been brave before, but only because nothing bad had ever happened to her. Maybe now – when she had come close to dying – she might be more sensible.

As we went on in the afternoon, we sailed out onto a broad stretch of water – maybe a river mouth or a wide sea loch – with a great mountain on the far side. I didn't think I had ever seen a mountain so huge. And it lay to the south-east of us, blocking us off from the direction of Embra.

"Which way now?" asked Rob. "Right or left?"

To the right lay hills and islands. The ocean must be somewhere beyond them. To the left, the loch ran inland, straight as a spear shaft. There were mountains on either side, but the loch itself stretched on beyond the horizon, with no end in sight.

"I've been here before," Ali said, suddenly interested. "I'm pretty sure we came here in the *Castle*. And the local people believed that you could sail up that loch and come out on the eastern coast of Scotland. Somebody's grandfather, or great grandfather, had done it long ago."

"But you didn't explore in that direction?" I said.

"No, because the winds were wrong. We sailed westwards instead, and came on a whirlpool between two islands, and nearly sank the ship."

"The winds are all right now," said Rob. "We could go north-eastward, and sail down the eastern coast to Embra. It is on the east coast, isn't it?"

"Of course it is." Ali gave him a look that meant, *Don't you know anything?*

"Well then. We'll go north-eastward, and turn southwards when we meet the sea."

At first it seemed like a good decision. The wind was with us and we made good speed along the loch. In the early evening, we began looking out for a place to spend the night – a house or maybe an island that would be safe from wild animals.

I thought I saw some houses ahead of us, near the shore. But, as we got nearer, we saw that they were just ruins. There wasn't enough shelter there for a cat.

An island, then? But there weren't any. The shores of the loch ran on straight ahead of us, into the far distance. And now the sun was sinking. We needed to find somewhere soon.

"What's that over there?" I said, pointing at some grey walls close to the waterside.

"It looks like the ruins of a castle," said Ali.

We sailed closer. There wasn't much left of the place – it looked as if it had been partly washed away by the sea. Some broken walls and the stump of a tower were left above the high-tide mark. Thick woods grew up on the landward side.

But it was better than nothing – a whole lot better. Inside the roofless tower, we built a fire, making sure we had plenty of spare wood to last through the night. There was no door, but we managed to bar the doorway with branches. As for the windows, they were just narrow slits, far too small to let dogs in.

We felt reasonably safe as we sat by the fire, with darkness falling outside, and the peaceful sound of water lapping. But there was something we should have thought about.

Firelight can be seen from a long way off. Firelight, glowing through the windows of a deserted building... It was certain to be noticed, if there were eyes to see.

Just before I lay down to sleep, I went to look out of the window. The rising moon made a ribbon of silver right across the loch. And across that bright pathway, something dark was moving. Something long and low, with a thin neck and a head like a snarling dog...

This was the thing that Donnie had seen! And it was heading straight towards us!

13
The thing

Without a word, I beckoned to Rob. He looked out, and his reaction was the same as mine.

"The monster of Ness!" he whispered.

Frantically I looked around at our fortress. It looked safe enough from dogs, but how would it stand up to a monster?

"Idiots!" said Ali, from the other window. "It's not a monster. It's a boat full of Norsemen!"

"What?"

I looked again. The thing, which was nearer now, seemed to change in front of my eyes. Now I could see that it was a boat, a long, black boat with a high, carved prow. With a row of oars on each side, it slid swiftly through the water.

This was what Donnie had tried to describe in the only way he knew. Not a monster... something even worse.

How many men were on board? They would surround us. We couldn't possibly fight them all off!

"We have to get out of here. Hide in the trees. Quick!" said Rob, grabbing at the branches that barred the door.

"But what if there are dogs... " Ali said in a faltering voice.

"Norsemen or dogs – take your pick," I said, helping Rob to open up the doorway.

We snatched up whatever possessions we could and dived out of the tower, into the shelter of the forest. It was pitch dark there. The moonlight couldn't reach through the thick branches overhead.

"Come on! Come on! Up the hill – further away," I said.

Dead branches tried to trip us, twigs stabbed us in the face and fear drove us on like the fiercest of wild dogs snapping at our heels. But suddenly Rob stopped running.

"The book, Jamie!" he hissed. "Where's the book?"

Oh, no! I'd been too busy making sure I had my bow and arrows with me. The book must still be in the tower.

"Leave it," I told him. "If the Norsemen catch you..."

But he was gone, charging down the hill again. This was even crazier than Ali's attempt to go back for the fish. He would get himself killed for the sake of a book!

"Let's get out of here," said Ali. But I couldn't. I had to see what happened to Rob.

The moonlit water rippled as the boat slid silently in, like a dark wave. Shadowy figures climbed out of it. They gathered on the shore, still silent, and the pale light glinted on axes and drawn swords. Then they crept through the trees towards the tower.

Another shadow, black against the firelight, leaped out of the doorway. It was Rob! They saw him but he was too quick for them. He darted into the trees.

A howl of fury went up. Some of them chased after him. The others surrounded the tower. Then they went in, and found nothing except our fire. The shouts became even louder. I couldn't understand the words, but I knew they were angry ones.

"Come on!" Ali urged me. "Rob will never find us in the dark. Get a move on!"

"The boat," I whispered. "If they find the boat, we're done for."

Some of the men snatched up burning branches from our fire. The flames shone on tall, broad-built fighting men, with cruel faces. They started spreading out through the woods and along the shore.

They found the boat, of course – we hadn't even tried to hide it. There was laughter, and then they took their axes and chopped it to bits. The Norsemen loved destroying things... and people.

Where was Rob? Ali was right – he hadn't a hope of finding us. The best thing would be to get well away from here, and hope to meet him again in daylight.

But the Norsemen were getting closer. They mustn't see us.

"Get down," I whispered to Ali. "Stay low."

We crouched in the undergrowth and tried to keep still. A Norseman came within a few yards of us. The flaming branch lit up his face, fierce and stern. He had fair hair, tied back like a horse's tail, and he carried a sharp-edged battle-axe. I shut my eyes, afraid to meet his gaze. But he strode past without seeing me.

Any moment I expected to hear a cry as the Norsemen captured Rob. But no sound came. After a long time, they gave up the search and went back down the hill. We could breathe again.

From a clearing in the trees, we watched the long, black boat heading out across the loch. Then it vanished in the dark shadow of the opposite shore.

Suddenly a hand grabbed me from behind. I almost yelled out – but it was Rob.

"You idiot!" I said. "You could have got yourself killed!"

"I didn't, though. And I got the book," he said triumphantly.

"Oh, great," said Ali. "Terrific. Shame you didn't manage to get the boat instead. What do we do now – walk to Embra?"

The summer nights are short, but that one seemed as long as midwinter. At last a glint of daylight appeared beneath a dark roof of cloud.

From our place on the hillside, as the light grew, we could see a long way up the loch. And on the far side there was something that made our hearts sink. A whole row of longboats – maybe ten or a dozen – lay in a sheltered bay. Half-hidden in the woods beyond, we could see some wooden cabins. The Norse raiders had built themselves a base here, in the heart of Scotland!

"But why would they want to settle here?" I asked.

"From here they can make raids on the east coast or the west coast, just as they like," Rob said.

"They could gather their ships here and make ready to attack Embra," said Ali. "They did that once before, in the days of the old king, but they lost the battle."

Even as we watched, another longboat was arriving from the north-east, sliding silently in with the dawn. We stepped back into the shelter of the trees, although we were too small to be seen, unless the Norsemen had eyes like eagles.

"If only the *Castle* had sailed this way," I said.

"Don't be stupid. Even the *Castle* couldn't fight off so many longboats," Ali said. "The Norsemen would board us while the cannons were being reloaded."

"We have to get to Embra and tell the king," Rob said. "Tell him to make ready for another battle."

Ali and I nodded in silent agreement.

I said, "We need another boat."

"Oh yes? Going to cut down trees and build a raft, are you?" Ali asked.

"Don't talk to me like I'm stupid," I said angrily. "If we walk along the shore, we'll eventually reach a place where people live and they'll have boats."

"I'm not so sure," said Rob. "Remember last night, when we saw the ruins of a village? I bet the Norsemen have made sure there's no one living within miles of here. I say we'd be better going overland."

"But we don't know the way," I said.

"South-eastwards," Rob said confidently.

"Yes, that's all very well when the sun's shining. But what if it's cloudy? We won't know which direction to go in. We could get lost in the mountains."

"It would still be safer than walking along the coast," Rob said. "That's the way the Norsemen will expect us to go, if they come looking for us."

"Come on then. What are we waiting for?" Ali asked.

We went up the hill. Soon we reached the upper fringes of the forest. Before us stood the mountains, bare of trees, wild and lonely. Steep slopes of heather and rock rose up to meet the grey, threatening sky. There were no paths – no sign that anyone ever came up here.

People said it was unlucky to venture into the high mountains. That was where the wild hunters were supposed to live.

"What's the matter?" Ali asked me. "Never seen mountains before?"

I told her about the wild hunters. "They think the mountains and all the deer belong to them. They kill people who go into their territory. It's bad luck to go anywhere near them."

"Oh, not more of this bad luck stuff. It's all a load of rubbish," she said angrily. "Why can't you see that?"

"Why can't *you* listen to anyone except yourself?" I said, equally angry. "You've brought us bad fortune ever since we first saw you. And now we've lost our boat, and we have to cross the mountains and put our lives in danger, all because of you. I wish we'd never met you!"

"Calm down, both of you," said Rob. "We've got enough problems without fighting amongst ourselves. Here – give each other the hand of friendship."

We shook hands because he asked us to, not because we were friends. I gripped Ali's hand as tightly as I could, and saw her wince in pain. But she said nothing.

"Now then – which way?" asked Rob.

We chose a narrow valley that led up between the hills. After a long, long climb, we reached a pass between two summits, and we could see what lay ahead.

Mountains and more mountains stretched far to the horizon, with the glint of water here and there in the valleys between. I couldn't see a single house or a thread of smoke rising from a cooking fire. It all looked empty and bleak.

"I don't see these wild hunters you keep talking about," said Ali.

"No, and you won't see them unless they want to be seen," I told her. "They can hide in the bracken like foxes."

"Come on," said Rob. "At least it's downhill from here. For a while, anyway."

And so we set out into the mountains.

14
Keep off!

By the end of the second day we were tired and footsore. Mountain walking was much harder work than sailing, or even rowing. We had no idea how far we had come, or how much further we still had to go.

We had spent the first night out in the open, with no fire. Even if there had been any wood to burn, we'd learned that it was dangerous to light fires. They made us too visible.

We took it in turns to stay awake that night, keeping guard. But no wild dogs or wild hunters came near us. As for the Norsemen, it was unlikely they would venture so far from their boats and from the sea.

It was strange, but I missed the sea. I had never been so far inland that you couldn't hear the sound of the waves in the distance. I didn't like being surrounded by mountains on every side – unknown mountains, empty of human life.

There were other kinds of life, though. We saw plenty of deer and, as our food supplies were running low, we decided to try for one. With my second arrow I shot a half-grown buck.

"We'll need a fire," I said, as I skinned it. "Unless you're planning on eating it raw."

"There's a forest in the valley, just ahead," said Rob.

We went into the thick of the forest, looking for a clearing where we could make a fire. If we waited until dusk, no one would see the smoke going up and the trees would hide the glow of burning branches. And we might need the fire, if there were wild dogs nearby.

In the bottom of the valley there was a river to give us drinking water. There was something else as well. Just upstream was a huge wall, which must once have gone right across the valley. But the river had broken through it, and a large section had fallen down. It was grey and sinister in the dim evening light.

"What's that?" I asked Rob.

"I don't know. It looks as if it's from the Old Times. It would be for collecting water, I think."

"But why on earth did they need so much water... A whole valley full?"

Nobody knew.

In the end, the best place we could find to build our fire was at the base of the enormous wall. This would give us protection from behind. We made a semi-circle of fire and gathered plenty of sticks to feed it through the night. Then we started roasting the deer meat.

It tasted wonderful. With full stomachs, we lay down to sleep, apart from Rob, who was taking the first turn on guard.

When it was my turn, he awakened me. I sat there, feeding the fire now and then, listening for any noise above the crackling of the flames. But it was hard to stay alert. I was tired... so tired...

All at once a horrendous crash made me sit up. Sparks were flying everywhere. Something had fallen onto one end of the fire - something big. It looked as if a chunk of the upper wall had come loose and fallen almost on top of us.

An accident? Or an attack?

I leapt up and had an arrow ready in an instant. But there was nothing to aim at - only the darkness all around. Everything was silent again.

"What happened?" The other two were awake, looking scared.

"A bit of the wall fell down - look!"

The chunk of grey rock was as big as a table. It would easily have killed us if it had landed any closer.

"There, you see?" I said. "We should have kept well away from this place. It's from the Old Times, and so was that castle tower. Both unlucky."

"Shut up," said Ali. "Listen."

We all listened, standing close against the wall in case more rocks came down. But nothing happened.

When daylight came, everything looked less frightening. If you stood further away from the great wall, you could see that the top of it was crumbling. Other big chunks had fallen down from time to time, and lay at the bottom like lumps of melting ice.

"It was just an accident," Rob said. "If somebody was trying to get us, why did they stop at one bit of rock?"

"Maybe they meant it as a warning," I said.

"Who did?" asked Ali.

"The wild hunters. They were telling us, 'Don't shoot the deer because they're ours'."

"It was an accident," Rob repeated. "Come on, let's get out of here."

We were all glad to get away from that place. Weary of mountains, we followed the river valley, which was leading eastwards – good, easy walking. You could almost think we were on a path. It was grassy, with young trees growing up, but here and there a hard, black surface showed through.

"It is a path," Rob said, when we came to the remains of a bridge over a stream.

"It's from the Old Times," Ali said. "But don't let Jamie know. He'll tell us it's unlucky."

She said that to annoy me, so I ignored her and kept walking. If we were on a path, it was quite a wide one - wide enough for two carts to pass each other all the way along. Very strange. But then, a lot of things from the Old Times are strange.

We walked all day along that path. The valley was widening and, as evening came on, we were glad to see stone-walled fields and a few houses.

At the first house there was an old man who looked at us suspiciously and wouldn't let us in. But the second house was more welcoming. The woman put some extra potatoes in the pot straight away. We ate with the family and told them about our journey.

We were disappointed to hear that Embra was still a long way away – maybe a week's walking. Nobody knew for sure.

"A week? By that time the Norsemen might have attacked," Rob said. "We have to get there as quickly as we can, to warn the king."

The people told us the best way to go, southwards through a mountain pass, following a road from the Old Times.

"It goes through the hunters' territory," said the man. "But they won't bother you, if you don't bother them. Most likely they'll let you pass through, and you won't even see them."

"But don't shoot any deer, whatever you do," his wife said. "And keep off the railway. The hunters don't like anyone walking on the railway."

What was the railway? I didn't ask, because I could see Ali already knew the answer, and was waiting for me to make myself seem like a fool.

The next day the weather didn't look good. There was a low ceiling of cloud, which hid the mountain tops. If we hadn't been in a hurry, we wouldn't have gone on with our journey. But time was scarce.

At least we had a road to follow. It was like before – a broad path, broken up now by plants growing through it, but still easy to make out. It climbed slowly, going up a river valley where there were no more houses, just grey hills on either side.

As well as the road, a different sort of path was climbing the valley. It looked stony and there were two long lines of metal, brown with rust. I decided that this must be the railway. The metal things were the rails.

It was odd that no one had removed any metal to make tools and weapons. Maybe they thought it would be unlucky. Or maybe they were afraid of the hunters.

The cloud level was getting lower, or rather we were climbing higher. And now we hit a problem.

There was a place where the road crossed to the other side of the valley. Long ago, there must have been a bridge, which the river had washed away. The river looked as if it could be forded, but it was very fast-flowing. If you lost your footing, it could easily sweep you away.

The railway, too, had a bridge. This one was in better shape, although the metal parts were very rusty. It looked as if we could use the railway bridge to cross the river, and then get back on our path again.

We argued about what to do. Ali said it was silly to get wet when we didn't need to.

"You're scared," I said to her. "You can't swim, can you?"

"No, you're the one that's scared. Just because somebody said to keep away from the railway. That is so stupid. I mean, what's going to happen?"

"The wild hunters. That's what could happen."

In the end Rob settled the argument. He said that if I didn't want to use the railway bridge, I didn't need to. I could walk or swim across the river. He and Ali would cross on the bridge.

I was angry because he'd taken Ali's side, not mine. But not so angry that I couldn't think straight.

"If the hunters see any of us on the railway, they'll be mad at all of us," I said.

Ali just smiled and looked around. "What hunters?"

Nothing seemed to be moving, apart from a few wisps of mist. Maybe it would be all right. Maybe the Wild Hunters were miles away, with no idea that we were here.

I decided to follow the others. With the river rushing beneath us, we stepped out onto the bridge.

15
The hunters

I was last in line. I had a nasty moment when a section of rusting metal fell away, almost under my feet. But I managed to get safely across.

Ali gave me a triumphant look.

"See? Nothing happened," she said. "Why don't we stay on the railway instead of the road? I'm pretty sure it goes all the way to Embra. The tracks have mostly been taken away, but you can still see where—"

Suddenly she stopped talking and put her hand up to her head. At the same instant I heard the whirr of an arrow, right past my ear. Someone was shooting at us!

"Get down! Down on the ground!" I cried.

There was nowhere to hide. As we lay sprawled on the railway line, I looked around frantically. Where had the arrows come from? There was a small wood not far ahead... and, out of the wood, a dozen people silently appeared. Each of them had an arrow ready.

The Wild Hunters! They looked wild all right. They wore clothes made of deerskin. The men were bearded and the women had long, matted hair. They looked more like animals than people.

"Now do you believe me?" I whispered to Ali.

The hunters came closer. Some of them stepped cautiously over the metal track, without touching it. When they had encircled us, one of them spoke.

"Get off the iron way," he ordered us, and aimed an arrow menacingly.

We scrambled to our feet and stood to one side of the railway. The circle of hunters gathered closer. Their lean faces looked as hostile as arrowheads.

"We should kill you," the leader said. His voice sounded rough, like an old knife blade, rusty with disuse. "Nobody is to walk on the iron way. The Old Ones will be angry."

"Don't kill us!" Ali cried. "We didn't know!"

"We're sorry," Rob said. "Let the anger of the Old Ones fall on us, not on you. If you let us go, we'll stay away from the rail... I mean, from the iron way."

"It's too late now," a young man said.

"Yes, too late. The Old Ones will have seen."

"Kill them! Kill them!"

"No, let them run, and we'll hunt them over the mountains!"

I said, desperately, "Don't kill us. We have a message for the king of Lothian. If you kill us, he'll never know that the Norse raiders are invading our country."

"What do we care about kings?" the leader said, proudly. "Or Norsemen? We are the hunters, the Wild Hunters! This is our land!"

Suddenly, one of the women spoke out. "We shouldn't kill these strangers. Look at them – they're only half-grown! We should take them to the great feast and let everyone see them. Maybe the Old Ones will give us a sign, telling us what we should do."

The others agreed with her. And so it came about that we were led into the mountains, away from the valley and the road.

Our weapons were taken from us. We were surrounded by the hunters. There was no chance of breaking away from them – they would have shot us before we had run ten paces.

Soon we were higher than the cloud level, climbing through thick mist. The hunters seemed to know where they were going, but I felt totally lost. I was hungry and thirsty, and the cold mist chilled me to the bone.

After a long climb, we started to descend again. A valley must lie below us, invisible in the mist. We stopped to drink from a spring, but nobody ate anything. The hunters were probably used to going all day without food.

We started moving again. They hurried us along, as if we were slowing them down from their normal pace.

They didn't speak much among themselves, and when I tried to talk to Rob, the leader silenced me with a frown.

Where were they taking us? What would happen?

At last we came down below the clouds again. We were in a narrow valley with forests at the bottom. The grey daylight was fading but, along the edges of the forest, I could see flickering flames. They looked like cooking fires – dozens of them. And between them were countless sleeping-shelters made of branches and bracken.

"I never knew there were so many hunters," Rob said, amazed.

The leader heard him. "This is our summer gathering," he said. "Tonight we're making a feast to honour the Old Ones."

I wished we were invited to the feast. My hunger was like a dull ache in my stomach. It got worse and worse as I smelt the food cooking.

We were kept under guard at the edge of the encampment. Then, as night fell, we were led forward to where the hunters were sitting in a great circle, with children and dogs at their feet. Firelight flickered on their faces.

They all stared at us, even the dogs, as we were pushed out into the centre of the circle. The hunters who had captured us, told everyone what we had done. There were cries of outrage, growing louder when another man sprang up to say that we had killed a deer two days before.

Rob muttered something in my ear. "The book, Jamie. Have you still got the book?"

I couldn't imagine what good it would do us, but I took it out of my pocket. Rob held it up so that everyone could see it.

"Do you know what this is?" he shouted. "It's a message from the time of the Ancestors... The Old Ones. Do you want to hear it?"

"Let me see that," an old man said. "Bring it here."

The man was so old that his beard was white and wispy, like the mist. He seemed to be some kind of chief. He took the book cautiously, as if it were a live snake that could kill him. While he was looking at it, the noise died down, and the hunters waited to hear what he would say.

"It is truly from the Old Times," he said, giving it back to Rob. "But I don't know the meaning of it. You are just a boy. Can you tell us what it means?"

Rob hesitated. In the dark, he couldn't read the book. I could tell he was trying to remember some of the things he'd read earlier.

"It says, don't murder people. Don't hate your enemies – be kind to them. And, if people do wrong and they're sorry, then don't take revenge on them."

"He's making it up," someone shouted. "The Old Ones never said that."

"No!" a woman cried. "The Old Ones hate our enemies!"

"The Old Ones are coming back one day, along the iron way," said the old chief. "And, when they come, they'll smash our enemies to pieces. They will be faster than lightning, angrier than thunder. Beware!"

"You're wrong," Ali shouted. "The Old Ones are never coming back. They were destroyed when the sea rose up. Their great cities were drowned. And parts of their iron way have been melted down to make swords and ploughs."

There was a sudden silence. I had the feeling she shouldn't have said that.

"Kill them! Kill them! Kill them!" The sound started as a low murmur and grew into a yell: "Kill them! Kill them!"

16
Hunted

Suddenly the woman who'd saved our lives stood up.

"Wait," she said. "What if the message truly comes from the Old Ones? If we kill their messengers, they'll be angry with us."

"Don't be a fool," someone shouted. "The boy made it all up. He mocked the Old Ones. He deserves to die!"

A long argument began. The leader tried to keep things in order, but his voice wasn't strong enough to be heard amidst the shouting.

"Set a test of strength," a young man called out. "Let the Old Ones decide what happens to the strangers."

"Yes! A test!" Other voices took up the cry.

"Throw them into the waterfalls at Salmon Leap!"

"Make them fight the wild dogs in the forest!"

The leader struggled to his feet and, seeing him, the crowd gradually fell silent again.

"Come here," he ordered us.

When we were lined up in front of him, he said, "I don't know what the Old Ones want us to do with you. So we'll let them decide. At dawn tomorrow, you are free to go. You must find your own way out of the mountains."

I looked at Rob, hardly daring to believe the old man's words. Were we really being set free?

But the old chief was still speaking. "At noon, our best hunters will set out on your trail. If they find you in the mountains, it's a sign from the Old Ones that you are to die. If you escape to the lowlands, it will mean you've found favour with the Old Ones."

Stupid of me to start hoping – for we would still face death, tomorrow or the next day. How could we possibly find our way out of the mountains with the wild hunters coming after us?

We were made to sit in the centre of the circle, like honoured guests. Then the feasting began. The hunters brought us roast venison and we ate hungrily. Maybe this would be our last ever meal.

After everyone had eaten, there was singing and storytelling, and a wild dance to the sound of a deerskin drum. Then a woman brought us some water. She was the same woman who had spoken up for us earlier.

She looked cautiously over her shoulder. But no one was interested in us now – everybody was watching the dancers.

"Listen to me," the woman whispered. "Go south from here. Go between the two lochs, and then over the mountains. Find the isles that were made by men, and my people will help you."

"Your people? What do you mean?" Rob asked her.

"Shhh!" She looked frightened.

"Aren't you one of the hunters?" Ali asked.

"I am – now. But I wasn't born to this life." Her dark eyes were full of sadness. "Ask my people if they remember Mairie."

"Do you want to go back to your own people?" Rob whispered. "If so, come with us. Show us the way."

"No, I can't. I have a husband and sons here. This is my life now."

She turned away and vanished in the darkness.

At dawn the hunters took us to the edge of the forest.

"No one will follow you until noon," the old chief said. "After that, what happens to you is up to the Old Ones to decide. Now go!"

We hurried into the trees. It was no use running – we would just get exhausted. We had to save our strength for the long day ahead.

There was a river in the valley-bottom, and all rivers run to the sea. If we simply followed the water, we would come out of the mountains sometime. But the hunters would expect us to do that. They could travel faster than we could. And they had dogs that would help them to hunt us down.

"I think we should do what the woman said," Rob told us. "Head south, find her people and hope that they help us."

Ali and I, for once, didn't argue. It would be a waste of time. And we didn't have any time to lose.

We went down river first of all, to leave a misleading trail. After a while, we doubled back, and waded up a side stream that was coming down from the hills to the south. A shoulder of the high ground hid us from the place where the hunters were gathered.

Although the rocks were slippery, we were glad to be climbing up the path of the stream. The water cooled us down, as well as washing away our scent. Already the sun was hot. The mists of yesterday had vanished.

At the top of the side valley, we came over the brow of a hill. Another valley lay spread before us.

"Two lochs," said Rob, sounding relieved. "She said to go between the two lochs. We're heading the right way."

"And then where? Over the mountains?" I said.

When I looked at those mountains, my heart sank. They were steep and high, forming a long barrier to the south. Ridge after ridge of grey rock and brown heather, with no trees to hide us from the sharp eyes of the hunters.

"How far will it be?" asked Ali.

"I don't know," Rob said. "Come on. We need to be over that first ridge before noon."

We made it. By noon, when the hunt was to begin, we had crossed the river between the two lochs and climbed the first ridge. But now we were starting to tire. The sun was beating down. There was no shade at all, and no water.

We rested on the ridge, lying down so as not to be seen against the sky. So far, there wasn't a sign of the hunters. With any luck, they would be following our false trail down the wrong valley.

Rob wouldn't let us rest for long. We set off again, down a short slope and up a much longer one. I tried to remember what the woman had said. Something about islands... but there was no water up here, so how could there be islands?

We struggled up to the top of the next ridge. I looked back, shading my eyes. Were there people on the far side of the two lochs? They were so far away, it was hard to tell.

Rob had seen them too. "We need to hurry," he said. "They're onto us."

Ali was weakening now. She was finding it harder to keep up with Rob and me. I suppose it wasn't her fault – after all, it was only ten days since she had been close to death. All the same, I started wondering what would happen if she couldn't go on.

We should leave her behind, I thought. There was no point in all three of us getting killed.

It was a tough haul up to the steepest ridge. On the far side were more hills, but they were lower. And beyond was the glint of sunlight on water. A long, narrow loch lay between the hills. Could that be where we would find the islands?

I couldn't see the hunters any more. They could be in one of the valleys behind us – we didn't wait to find out.

The sun moved westwards. We struggled on, hot and sweating, surrounded by clouds of insects. In a valley, we drank hurriedly from a peat-brown stream. There was no time to stop and enjoy it, because now we could see the hunters at the top of the highest ridge.

They weren't even trying to stay hidden. They must be certain they could catch us. To them, this was probably a kind of sport – they were enjoying the hunt. And they would enjoy the kill even more.

"Come on! Come on!" Rob urged Ali. "Not much further now."

She was breathing hard. "Go on," she gasped. "Don't wait for me."

"No," he said stubbornly. "We'll stick together. Come on! You can do it!"

We fought our way up one last hill. Now we could see the whole length of that loch, red in the sunset. Here and there along the edge, there were islands... no, not islands... buildings. Round houses that seemed to be built on stilts in the water.

These must be the islands made by men. But could we reach them in time? And would anyone help us?

We went down through trees and over a wall into fields. There were sheep and goats near the water. Two girls with dogs were rounding them up, herding them onto a wooden pier that led to a group of island-houses. The girls stared at us as we came closer.

"Help us," I gasped. "The wild hunters are after us."

The smaller girl looked scared. The bigger one smiled at us, as if this sort of thing happened every day.

"Come with us," she said.

We followed the last of the sheep onto the wood-fenced pier. I wished the sheep would move faster. Any moment now, the hunters might appear.

Halfway across, the girls stopped. They started turning a handle, which wound a rope around an axle. A section of the wooden pier began to tip upwards, as if on hinges. Now there was a gap, too wide to jump, between the fixed parts of the pier.

Very clever, I thought. The man-made island was truly an island now, and it was more than a bow-shot away from land. Unless the hunters could build a boat, we were safe from them... for the moment.

17

The people of the loch

The animals were sent to one island; we were led to another. It was built on wooden poles, well above the water. There was a round house, made of wood and woven reeds, with a pointed roof of thatch.

The girls called for their father and he came to the door. Rob started to explain about the hunters. But by now Ali had come to the last of her strength. Her legs gave way under her and she collapsed on the floor.

"Bring her indoors," the man said.

Between us we carried her in. A woman showed us to a couch where she could lie down and brought us all some water. It felt so good to sit down, to stop running away and be at peace.

The peace didn't last for long, though. Soon we could hear voices shouting from the lake shore.

"Send them out! They're ours!"

"The Old Ones have given them into our hands!"

"Give them to us! If you don't, the Old Ones will be angry!"

The man of the house went to the door again.

"Tell them you don't know what they're talking about," I urged him. He looked at me gravely.

"I must not tell lies," he said. "But I'll do what I can to help you."

"Aren't you afraid of the hunters?" Rob asked.

"We've lived in peace with them since my grandfather's time. We have an agreement - if we don't hunt their deer, they don't steal our sheep. Most of the time they stick to it."

He went out and we heard him talking to the hunters across the water. He asked them why they were chasing us, and they explained.

"We were close on their trail," one of the hunters said. "The Old Ones must have meant us to catch them. Don't anger the Old Ones!"

The man said, "You know I don't fear the Old Ones. I follow Jesus, and he tells me to help anyone in trouble. These children were strangers and we took them in. If we sent them away, it would be like sending away Jesus himself."

Rob looked surprised. "What he's saying is written in your book," he whispered to me. "These people must believe in the God of the book!"

I looked around at the people of the house. They seemed perfectly ordinary to me. There were about a dozen of them, all different ages. They were listening intently to the argument outside, and I realised that we had put their lives at risk by coming here.

The argument went on for a long time. Neither side would give in. At last, as dark was falling, the hunters made camp in the field. The man of the house came back indoors, looking anxious.

"How many of them are there?" asked a woman.

"Eight. But by tomorrow there will be more of them."

Someone said, "This could be the start of a war between their people and ours."

"We don't want that," Rob said. "We don't want to put you in danger."

I said, "If you can let us have a boat, we'll get away from here during the night."

The man of the house liked this idea, I could tell. He was torn between helping us and protecting his family.

"We have canoes tied up under the house," he said. "You can have one. You could paddle over to the far side of the loch. But don't go yet. Wait until it gets really dark."

"And have some food first," a woman said.

She gave us bread and cheese and we ate hungrily, in between answering questions. When we mentioned that we were on our way to Embra, there was a murmur of dismay.

"It's a wicked city, Embra," someone said.

"What's wicked about it?" Ali demanded.

"Everyone lives for their own pleasure. They've forgotten the name of God."

The man said, "That's why our great grandfathers brought us out of the city. God told them to settle here, in this valley."

"Do you have a book that tells you about your God?" Rob asked him.

The man looked at him blankly. "What's a book?"

I took out the book and let the people look at it, by the light of a tallow lamp. Then Rob started reading one of the stories about Jesus.

"We know that story," a girl said, and she told him how it ended. She must have learned it through hearing it many times, as I had learned Granny's story of the Ancestors. But, when Rob read some more of the book, it was obviously new to his listeners. They heard it with wonder.

An old woman said, "I think my grandmother used to tell us that. But I'd forgotten all about it."

"There may be a lot more that we've forgotten," another woman said. "I wish we had this book!"

"It's no good unless you can read it," I told her.

Rob said, "We're taking it to Embra with us. There are people in Embra who can read. Maybe they'll listen to what it says."

"And maybe not," Ali muttered.

"What's the quickest way to get out of the mountains?" I asked. "If we can get as far as the lowlands, the hunters will stop chasing us."

A young man spoke up. He was tall and dark-haired, with a friendly, open face. He looked like an older brother of the two shepherd girls.

He said, "Take a boat down the river. That's the quickest way."

"No! It's far too dangerous," someone else said. "Think of the rapids!"

"The rapids aren't too bad at this time of year," the young man said. "I could go with you. I know the first bit of the river – I've been fishing there."

His eyes were alight with excitement. Oh, no... not another one like Rob, keen to go out adventuring!

But we needed his help, especially when it became clear that we would have to take two boats, not one. The canoes, we were told, would only hold two people each. The young man – Malcolm was his name – would take Ali in his canoe. Rob and I would have to try and manage the other one.

We had to climb down a rope ladder to reach the canoes. It was very dark under the house. That was all to the good – I had been afraid that, when we set out across the loch, the hunters would see us in the moonlight.

I sat down inside the canoe, which built on a wooden frame, with a skin of leather. It felt very low in the water and quite unsteady. When Rob sat down in front of me, it wobbled even more. We each had a wooden paddle. I wished we had a proper boat with oars and a sail.

In the second canoe, Malcolm and Ali were just dark shapes. Another dark shape was Malcolm's father, who was on the rope ladder, ready to untie our moorings. "God be with you," he said quietly.

We glided out from under the house, on the side away from the shore. At that very moment, a cloud slid over the moon. It couldn't have been better timed. There was no sound from the hunters' camp – they never saw us go.

After paddling across the loch for a while, Rob and I began to get the hang of things. Malcolm stayed close beside us. At last we bumped against the poles of another island-house.

"We'll stay here tonight," Malcolm said. "We can't go down river in the dark."

I wondered what the people of the house would think. They must be in bed by now. They probably knew Malcolm, but the rest of us were complete strangers, arriving in the darkness, without any warning.

Amazingly, they let us in. They made us welcome, just as the others had done. We were given more food and a place to sleep.

"These are good people," Rob whispered to me. "They do what it says in your book, even though they've never read it. Weird!"

"Yeah. Go to sleep, Rob."

I sank into a deep, exhausted sleep. But it hardly seemed a moment before Malcolm was shaking me awake again. Daylight was creeping in at the window.

"It's time to go down the river," he said. "Are you ready?"

18
The river

We ate a hurried breakfast. Looking out, I realised that I couldn't even see the far side of the loch. There was a mist filling the whole valley. That was good – the hunters wouldn't be able to see us set out.

But this thought worried Rob. He said, "They'll think we're still in the other house. They might attack it."

Ali said, "How? It's on an island, remember."

"I bet they could find a way. And then, what would they do to your people, Malcolm?"

"They'd be very angry," Malcolm said. "Especially when they found out that you'd escaped. They would want to kill my family."

"So we have to show the hunters that we're not there any more," Rob said. "We ought to make them come after us and leave your people alone."

I knew he was right. That was what we ought to do – but I didn't want to take the risk. We were safe now. We'd got away free. Why throw it all away?

Looking at Ali, I was pretty sure she felt the same as me. We were both afraid... afraid of being hunted down... afraid of dying.

But I said nothing. I didn't want to look like a coward. And Ali, too, was silent, as we got into the canoes and paddled out into the mist.

Slowly, the opposite hillside loomed towards us through the drifting whiteness. Now we could see Malcolm's house, and the hunters in the field beyond. Three of them were at the end of the pier, as if guarding it. The others were coming down from the woods, dragging long branches behind them.

"You see? They're going to try and get in," said Rob.

"We mustn't go too close," I breathed. "Keep out of arrow range."

"Hey!" Rob shouted at the top of his voice. "We're over here!"

They all heard him. Instantly, the nearest ones took aim at us, but their arrows fell harmlessly into the water.

"That ought to do it. They'll leave my family alone now," said Malcolm, sounding relieved.

We paddled off into the mist again, until we could see the opposite shore of the loch. Then Malcolm told us to turn left, heading down the loch towards its outlet, which was a river. The river would carry us out of the mountains.

"The hunters are sure to guess we're going that way," said Ali. "Can they get to the river before us?"

"I don't think so. There are thick woods further down on that side of the loch," Malcolm said. "They won't be able to move too fast – not like over the hills."

All the same, we paddled faster. My arms were already getting tired, and the loch seemed endless. We passed two more of the island-houses, but didn't stop.

The mist was slowly lifting. Now I could see that the loch was getting narrower. To reach the river, we would have to go close to the opposite shore. What if the hunters were ready for us? Out on the open water, there was nowhere to hide from their arrows.

But Malcolm had been right. They hadn't managed to get there before us; we entered the river safely. I felt the current seize hold of the boat, and I stopped paddling for a moment, glad to rest my aching arms.

The river was broad and fast-flowing, with woods on both sides. Soon we left the loch behind, and I started to relax slightly. This was easy... even easier than sailing.

Then Malcolm called out, "Get ready for the rapids – just around the next bend."

I could see rough water ahead, where the river tumbled down over rocks. It was white with foam and the sound of it roared in my ears.

Holding grimly onto my paddle, I tried to help Rob steer after Malcolm's canoe. But the water was stronger than we were. It swirled around us, dragged us sideways and scraped us against the rocks.

I was terrified. I was sure we were about to capsize, and all kinds of memories ran through my head. Grandad... the storm... the huge waves... No! I don't want to die!

Then at last it was over. We came through into calmer water, still upright, with the boat still afloat. I sighed with relief.

"That wasn't so bad," said Rob. "I don't know what all the fuss was about. Are there any more rapids, Malcolm?" He actually looked hopeful as he said it.

"I hope not," said Ali. "Because our boat's leaking."

"Oh. Is it a bad leak?" asked Rob.

We pulled the canoes onto the river bank and turned them over to let the water out. Now we could see the damage to Malcolm and Ali's canoe. A seam had begun to split, just below the waterline.

"We can still use the canoe," Malcolm said. "For a while, anyway. But we'll have to stop now and then to drain the water out."

"Maybe we should leave the boats and walk," I suggested.

But Malcolm said it would be quicker by canoe, and harder for the hunters to follow us.

"We must have left them behind by now, surely," said Ali.

"The ones we saw - yes. But that was just a few of them. How many were sent out to look for you?"

We didn't know.

"There might be more hunters further down the valley," said Rob. "They know we're trying to get to the lowlands. All they have to do is lie in wait for us."

"Then we should leave the valley and cross the mountains instead," I said, and we argued for a bit.

"Come on. We're wasting time," said Rob. "I say we let Malcolm decide. He knows this land, and we don't."

Malcolm said the canoes would be our best chance, unless the leak got really bad. So we set off down the river again.

At least there were no more rapids for a good long way. The river was calmer, winding back and forth across the valley. Thick forests grew on either side – perfect for an ambush. When we had to stop again to bale out Malcolm's canoe, I stood guard, although without my bow there wouldn't be much I could do if we were attacked.

Around midday we reached a place where our river joined another one, running southwards through a broad valley.

"How long until we get to the lowlands?" Rob asked Malcolm. But he couldn't say – we had already gone further down river than he had ever been before.

In this new valley there was something that made my heart sink. It was a raised ridge of earth, running along the side of the river. Where a side stream came down to join the river, there was the skeleton of a bridge from the Old Times. We had reached the railway again.

Ali was pleased. "At least we know we're back on the right path," she said.

I thought it was a bad omen. The railway had already brought us bad luck once – it might do the same again.

As we went on through the afternoon, the leak got worse. We had to stop several times to drain the water out. Ali and Malcolm had wet clothes from sitting in a pool of water. Luckily it was a warm day – the mist had gone and the sun was hot.

The broad valley narrowed. Steep, forest-covered hills closed in on either side. It almost looked as if we were going deeper into the mountains, apart from one thing.

"The sea," I said. "I can smell the sea."

"Well, I can't," said Ali. "You're imagining it."

I didn't argue with her. I knew that smell, and it made my heart feel lighter. Surely we must be close to the lowlands now.

Rob was looking worried. "What's the matter?" I asked him.

"I was just thinking – if I was a hunter, this would be a great place to set an ambush for us."

We had to stop yet again. Because of what Rob had said, we chose an island in the middle of the river. It was still within a bow-shot of the banks, but it seemed safer... at first.

We hadn't even got the boats out of the water when Rob cried out. An arrow had hit him on the shoulder.

"They've seen us!" he gasped.

"Quick, get back in the canoes!" Malcolm shouted. "It's our only chance!"

19

The cave

I paddled down river as fast as I could. Rob was trying to pull out the arrow that had hit him.

"At least there was only one of the hunters," he gasped.

"How do you know?"

"Because if there had been a gang of them, we'd all be dead by now." He moaned in pain.

Malcolm said, "The hunters are like ants. Where there's one, there are always more nearby. Can you hear that bird call? That's a signal they use."

"What are we going to do?" cried Ali. "This canoe won't stay afloat much longer!"

I looked around desperately. Steep forests to the left. More forests to the right and, close to the shore, partly hidden by trees, the railway. There was no help in sight.

And now the river, which had helped us for so many miles, seemed to have turned against us. It was hard work to paddle against the flow of water.

"There's an incoming tide," I said. "We can't be far from the sea."

But would we make it? We were all exhausted. Malcolm's boat was close to sinking. And Rob still had half an arrow in his shoulder – his shirt was drenched in blood.

"We're going to have to land," said Malcolm.

We chose the right-hand side of the river because the arrow had come from the opposite shore. Of course, there could be hunters on this side too. We abandoned the canoes at the waterline and struggled ashore through thick, brown mud.

"The railway! Make for the railway," said Ali.

"Why?"

"Because the hunters don't like going near it. And it'll be quicker than trying to get through the trees."

She was right. The stony path of the railway had become partly overgrown, but it looked much easier ground than the steep forest. All the same, I didn't like it. It would bring bad luck – I was sure of that.

Rob had lost a lot of blood. I helped him along, with his good arm over my shoulder. He was muttering something. After a while I realised that he wasn't talking to himself, or to me.

"Help us, God! Please help us!"

I joined in silently. Please help us, God... whoever you are... if you're listening...

One good thing about the railway – it ran level. The Ancestors had cut through hills and filled in valleys to make a smooth path. They never knew how grateful we would be, long after they were all dead.

But, even on level ground, Rob wouldn't be able to walk much further. He was losing strength. I could feel it.

From behind came that bird-call signal, much closer than before. Any moment now, the first arrows would come out of the trees.

Suddenly, Ali called out, "Look! The railway goes into a cave!"

Ahead of us there was a hill. And the railway headed straight towards it, first in its own narrow valley, then into a dark hole in the hill. It looked frightening – like a black mouth that could swallow us whole. But where else could we go?

"Maybe the hunters... won't follow us in there," Rob gasped. And he tried to go faster, as if he'd started to hope we had a chance. But then a spent arrow clattered against the rails behind us. The hunters were getting close.

"You go on," Malcolm said. "I'll wait here and see if I can hold them off."

"No!" Rob gasped. "They'll kill you!"

"Maybe. That's in God's hands." His face was quite calm. "Now, get going. Hurry!"

Between us Ali and I half-carried Rob towards the cave mouth. Malcolm stood at the entrance to the narrow valley, waiting for the hunters. He had no weapons, nothing to fight them with. It was the bravest thing I had ever seen.

As we got nearer to the cave, I heard angry shouts from behind. But nobody fired at us. Looking back, I saw Malcolm facing a crowd of hunters.

When we were far enough in to be hidden by the darkness, I told Ali to stay with Rob. Then I slipped back towards the entrance. I'd noticed a sort of archway in the side of the cave, just big enough for a man to hide in. From here I could see what was happening to Malcolm.

The hunters were all around him now. Threatening him with spears, they made him move off the railway line.

"Why did you help the strangers?" one of them shouted. "The Old Ones are angry with them!"

"They deserve to die, and so do you!" another one cried.

Malcolm said, "Kill me, if you must kill someone. But let the strangers go. They're just children! Take my life instead of theirs!"

He held his hands out to prove he had no weapons. For a moment the hunters looked taken aback. It seemed they admired his courage – and none of them wanted to be the first to attack him.

But then that hate-filled chant started up. "Kill him! Kill him! Kill him!" And one man stepped forward, spear in hand.

Malcolm turned to face him. Surrounded by enemies, with death just a spear-length away, he didn't even flinch. The hunter balanced his weapon and took aim... I couldn't watch any more.

I ran back towards the others. "They're killing him!"

"We should go out there," said Rob.

"If we do, we'll all die," I said.

Our voices sounded strange in the darkness... a hollow sound, like a ghost might make. It was frightening – hardly human.

"Listen to that!" gasped Rob, and again came that eerie sound.

"Turn around," he whispered. "Shout as loudly as you can."

Facing towards the cave mouth, I gave a long, loud, wordless howl. The hunters heard it. Every face turned towards the cave.

"Do not kill him!" I yelled. "Send him to us! We are the Old Ones. We will deal with him!"

With terror on their faces, the hunters backed away from Malcolm. They jabbed at him with their spears, making him head for the cave. He staggered towards us, both hands pressed against his side. He had been wounded... but at least he was alive.

As soon as he was close to us, Ali shouted, "Go home! The Old Ones are pleased with you!"

The hunters scurried off into the trees. But one or two of them looked back, as if they'd started to get suspicious of the strange voices.

"We'd better not go out there. Not yet, anyway," I whispered.

"I think there's daylight at the far end of the cave," said Ali. "Maybe we can get out that way."

Helping Rob and Malcolm along, we stumbled through the darkness. Ice-cold water dripped on us from the roof. The ground was tricky, with fallen rocks and rusty metal underfoot. More than once, I felt Rob was ready to give up. But we urged him on.

Slowly, the tiny point of light ahead of us grew bigger. At last we came out into daylight, moving cautiously in case there were hunters on this side of the hill.

"I have to sit down," Rob gasped.

"Just a few more steps. Then you can rest."

A few more steps, though, changed everything. A view opened up in front of us – a broad river estuary, with low hills to the south of it. There were farms, fields and a town at the river's edge. No more bleak mountains, no more dark forests.

"Is this the lowlands?" I asked. "Is that Embra?"

Gazing around, Ali said, "I've no idea where we are. But that looks like one of the king's ships."

The ship was moored in the river channel. A banner at the mast-top caught the wind, and we saw it clearly – a fierce, snarling beast in red and yellow.

"That's a ship of the fleet, all right," said Ali. "There'll be a doctor on board. And they can take us to Embra."

"Will they listen to us?" I said doubtfully.

For Ali no longer looked like a sailor of the king's fleet. Her uniform was ripped and bloodstained. Her face was spattered with mud.

"Of course they'll listen," she said, impatiently. "We have urgent news for the king. Come on! Not far now before we're home and dry!"

20
Not afraid

Ali hailed the ship and demanded to see the captain. "We have a message for the king," she shouted. "It's vitally important."

At first the sailors laughed at her. But, after some arguing, a boat was sent out for us and they rowed us across to the ship. Rob couldn't manage to climb up the ladder to get on-board. He had to be hoisted up using a rope and pulley, like a sack of grain.

"Get the ship's doctor," Ali cried. "We have two wounded men here! And, now, take me to the captain!"

"Yes ma'am. At once, ma'am," a sailor said mockingly. But he led Ali and me to the captain's cabin all the same.

We told the captain about the Norsemen. He listened intently. His ship had been exploring the east coast of Scotland, just as the *Castle* was doing on the west coast.

"And everywhere we went, people told us that the Norsemen were getting bolder. But we never saw them," he said.

"No wonder, if they have a hidden base miles from the open sea," said his second-in-command.

"There's no time to lose. We must set sail at once," the captain said.

"For Embra?" asked Ali. "Can we come with you?"

"Of course you'll come with us. The king will want to hear this from your own mouth."

"How long will it take us to get there?" I ventured to ask.

"Two days with this wind. Sooner, if we get a bit more of a breeze. So let's get moving!"

He strode out on deck and started shouting orders. At once the great ship sprang into life. Sailors appeared from below and ran up the rigging, ready to unfurl the huge sails. I watched, fascinated. But Ali had seen it all before.

"Come on, let's see if Rob and Malcolm are all right," she said.

We went down to a lower deck and found the doctor's cabin, which had a red cross on the door. Inside, Rob was lying on a table. The doctor was cutting out the arrow-head from his shoulder. Rob lay without moving, eyes closed.

He was dead, then? I stared in horror, but Ali told me not to be so daft. "The doctor's put him to sleep, that's all," she said.

The doctor said, "This lad's going to be fine. I'll just stitch up the wound before he comes round again."

"What about Malcolm?" I asked. But the doctor didn't reply.

Malcolm was still awake, lying on a bed. He had been stabbed in the side, and his face showed how much pain he was in.

"Malcolm, you were so brave," Ali said to him. "You risked your life for us."

"We would all be dead if it wasn't for you," I said.

Malcolm's face was as grey as a stone. When he spoke, his voice came in gasps. "I was just... doing what Jesus said. Following my Lord. He laid down his life... for his friends."

"But you're not going to lay down your life," Ali said fiercely. "You won't die!"

"I'm not afraid... to die," he whispered.

"That's good, but it's not going to happen." She gripped hold of his hand. "The doctor will make you well again."

His face twisted. He was struggling to talk again, or to pray. "Even though I walk through... valley of death... I won't be afraid, because you are with me, Lord. Surely goodness and mercy... all my days... and I'll live in the house of the Lord... for ever."

"Doctor! Can't you hurry up?" Ali cried.

"Yes, yes. I'm coming. I'll give him something that will ease the pain." He poured some liquid from a bottle onto a piece of cloth, and held it to Malcolm's nose and mouth.

"Better. That's better," Malcolm murmured, and his eyes began to close.

The doctor went back towards Rob. I followed him.

"Is Malcolm going to die?" I asked him, as quietly as I could.

He sighed. "I'm afraid there's not much I can do for him. He's bleeding internally. All I can do is help him to bear the pain."

Malcolm moved restlessly on his bed. He was whispering something. "Peace I leave with you... my peace I give you. Don't let your heart be troubled. There are many rooms in my father's house... "

"What's he talking about?" asked Ali.

"I don't know, but they sound like words from my book."

"The book," Malcolm said, and suddenly his eyes opened wide. "You still have the book?"

"Yes." Amazingly, after all we'd been through, it was still in my pocket.

"You must take it to the king. Promise me... the king must see it. Very important... Do you hear me?"

"I hear you, Malcolm. I promise I'll take it to the king."

He smiled. His eyelids closed, and he drifted off into sleep. A calm sleep, a peaceful sleep. Nothing disturbed him, not even when the ship heeled over and the doctor's tray of knives crashed to the floor.

During the evening, we kept watch beside his bed. But he never woke up again. As it was growing dark outside, he took his last breath.

"He wasn't scared of dying," Ali said. "Why not? Was he stupid or something?"

Her voice sounded harsh. But her eyes were full of tears.

All the next day we sailed on south-eastwards, then south. The wind was getting stronger all the time, and the sailors said we might reach Embra before nightfall. I hoped they were right – it looked to me as if a storm might be on the way.

In the afternoon, Rob struggled up on deck. He was feeling tired and weak, but he hated being below decks. It made him feel seasick, he said.

We told him what had happened to Malcolm. He was quiet for a long time. At last he said, "We hardly even knew him."

"He was a good friend, though," I said. "What was it he said, Ali? Something about following Jesus... giving up his life for his friends."

"He wasn't afraid," said Ali. "That's what I can't understand. *Everybody's* afraid of dying."

As if to underline her words, a mighty gust of wind made the ship heel over further. We all grabbed onto the rail.

"In your book," Rob said, "it talks about people living on after their death. Living in heaven – God's house. Where there's no more sorrow or pain or death. That's why Malcolm wasn't scared... he knew where he was going."

"What if he was wrong, though?" asked Ali. "I mean, who knows for sure? Everybody believes in different things. Like the hunters believe the Old Ones are coming back, and Jamie believes in good and bad luck, and Malcolm's people believe in the God of the book. They can't all be right, can they?"

I thought she had a point. "What do you believe in, then?" I asked her.

"I believe in myself. Doing what I want to do. That's all," she said. "What about you, Rob?"

"I'm not sure," he said slowly. "But the more I look at that book, the more I believe in the God it talks about. The God who loves us like a father."

A sudden shout came from the masthead. "Embra in sight! Embra on the starboard bow!"

Soon we could see it too – a dark smudge of smoke on the horizon. At first I thought the Norsemen must have got there before us and set the city aflame. But Ali said it always looked like that. The smoke came from hundreds of cooking stoves, and the smell came from thousands of people.

"What smell?" asked Rob.

But, as we sailed closer, we could smell it all too clearly. The wind brought it to us... the smell of smoke and the stink of a dunghill.

"You'll get used to it after a while. You'll hardly notice it," Ali said confidently. "Welcome to Embra!"

21

Journey's end

The storm that had been brewing all day was about to break. But the ship had come safely to harbour.

"Come with me," said the captain. "We must take your news to the castle."

The only way to get there was by boat, for the castle was on an island. According to Ali, there were several islands making up the city of Embra. It was a huge place, fifty times bigger than the only town I had ever been to before.

The rowing boat landed us on a stony slipway. I helped Rob get out. He was still feeling weak, but he had refused to let us leave him on the ship.

Gazing around, I saw that the old tales were right – in Embra there were houses taller than trees. They were joined together in two long rows, like two cliffs. A broad, stony path lay between them, leading up the hill towards the castle.

It was getting dark by now. Here and there on the walls strange lights suddenly shone out, without anyone lighting them. They didn't flicker like candles or tallow lamps, but burned steadily. How could that happen?

"Come on, Jamie. Don't stand there staring like a village idiot," said Ali.

"I don't see all the hundreds of people your Uncle Davie talked about," I said to Rob, for the street was almost empty. The wind howled down it, blowing rain straight into our faces.

"I suppose they're at home," he said. In a low voice he added, "I wish I was too."

"What? But we're in Embra! The place you always wanted to come to!"

"Not like this. I didn't want it to be like this." With one hand he touched his bandaged shoulder. "I thought I would be like Uncle Davie, and fight for the king."

"Maybe you will, when you get better."

"*If* I get better."

I knew why he was worried. The wound was in his right shoulder. If it didn't heal well, he might never again be skilful with a sword. He would be crippled for life, like his uncle.

Ali said, "Don't worry. We have good doctors here in Embra."

I felt like telling her that the doctors weren't all-powerful – if they were, Malcolm would still be alive. But I managed to keep my mouth shut.

We came out into an open space at the end of the street. And now the castle loomed over us like a mountain, wall behind wall, tower above tower. Below, in the darkness, I could hear waves breaking against rocks.

There was a gatehouse, with armed men on guard.

"Halt! Who goes there?" one of them demanded.

"Captain Ewan, of the king's ship, the *Lion*. I have an urgent message for the king."

Ali pushed herself forward. "Ali Monroe, of the king's ship, the *Castle*."

"Robert Macdonald, son of the chief of Insh More," said Rob.

"Jamie Brown," I said flatly, wishing I had some kind of rank or title. The guards were staring at us, clearly wondering what we were doing here.

"Young as they are, the king will want to speak to all three of them," said the captain. "I guarantee it. Let them pass."

One of the guards led us up a steep road inside the walls and through another gatehouse. There were more of the strange, bright lamps to light our way. But suddenly, all the lights flickered and died. We were left in pitch-blackness.

The guard swore. "The power's gone. The wind turbines can't take a gale like this," he said.

He went back to the gatehouse and returned with a candle lantern. It lit the path ahead of us, but we couldn't see much of the castle itself. It was enormous – that was all you could say for certain. On the higher levels the wind blew fiercely, as if it wanted to snatch us away into the night.

At last we came to a huge door. We had to wait outside while a servant was sent to the king, asking if the captain could see him. It was late by now. I was expecting we would be sent away until the morning.

But the servant came back quite quickly. Yes, the king would see us.

We were led through vast rooms, dimly lit by candles. I caught glimpses of huge stone fireplaces and walls of polished wood. There was something soft, like thick cloth, covering the floors, so that our feet made little noise. From the walls, painted people looked down at us.

"This must be the royal palace!" Ali whispered. "I never thought I'd see the inside of it!"

We went up some stairs and into a much smaller room. A fire was burning on the hearth. Compared with the great, empty halls, the room felt warm and welcoming. Two men, one young and one older, sat at a table. The captain bowed to the younger one.

Was this the king, then? His Royal Majesty, King Andrew of Lothian? I thought he should be wearing a crown and rich robes, not ordinary clothes. And his face should be proud and haughty. Instead, he looked friendly and interested. He reminded me of Rob's eldest brother.

"Bow down, Jamie," Rob hissed in my ear. I made an awkward bow, never having learned this kind of thing. The older man gave me a disapproving stare.

"Captain Ewan, it's good to see you," King Andrew said. "You know Sir Kenneth, my chief counsellor. But what brings you here on such a stormy night? And who are your young friends?"

"Your Majesty, these youngsters bring news of the utmost danger. The Norsemen are gathering again. They're not just making raids on the coast and then returning home. They have actually set up a base deep in the heart of Scotland."

We had to tell what we'd seen in as much detail as we could. The king listened intently, asking many questions. It was clear that our answers disturbed him.

The chief counsellor brought out a big, ancient-looking book, and turned the pages with great care.

"These are maps from the Old Times," he said. "Inaccurate now, of course – the coastline has completely changed. But, until the royal mapmakers finish their work, these are the best maps we have. Can you show us where you saw the Norse settlement?"

I knew it was pointless for me to try – I couldn't even read the names on the map. But Rob leaned over it, looking carefully.

"This loch here, Loch Ness," he said, pointing, "could be part of the place called the Straits of Ness. It's now an open-ended channel cutting right across the country. And I believe we saw the Norsemen here... or maybe here... " he continued, pointing at places on the map.

Ali said, "From there, they can raid the east or the west coast. Or even get ready to attack Embra, like they did before."

"Yes," said King Andrew. "My father defeated them outside the city ten years ago. He thought they would never trouble us any more. But it seems they've grown strong again."

"We must be ready for them!" said Sir Kenneth.

"I can't thank you enough for bringing me this news," the king said to the three of us. "You will stay here, as my guests. My captains may need your knowledge when they plan how to take action."

He called two servants and told them to find us rooms for the night. It was clear that our part in the meeting was at an end. But suddenly I remembered something.

The book! Malcolm had wanted the king to have the book. And I might never have another chance like this, face to face with the king.

All the same, I hesitated. I didn't want to trouble the king when he had to prepare to meet an invasion. What would he think of me? I would look like a fool. And I hated that.

But Malcolm... it was Malcolm's last wish before he died. "Very important," he had said. And I had promised...

The servant was ushering us towards the door. Taking my courage in both hands, I turned back towards King Andrew.

"There's something else, Your Majesty. I have a book here, and our friend Malcolm – he's not here now, he's dead – he wanted you to have it." I placed the book on the table. "I know you won't have time to read it now. But Malcolm said it's very important."

"Thank you," the king said. "To me, all books are important. They may all contain knowledge that would otherwise be lost."

"But this one is special," said Rob.

"I will make sure I read it, as soon as time allows." He smiled at us. "And now, good night."

Rob and I were given a bedroom high up in the castle. The servants offered to bring us some food, but we were too tired to feel hungry.

I sank down on one of the beds. It was made of something much softer than heather or straw and it had curtains hung around it to keep out the draughts. But suddenly I had a longing for my own bed at home, far away.

Rob went to the window and unfastened the shutters. The wind came roaring into the room, making the candles flicker. He stared down into the darkness.

"What are you doing?"

"Just having a look at the city."

I went to join him at the window. The moon, half-hidden by ragged clouds, showed us the isles of Embra, laid out like a map. Walls and turrets, lighted windows, dark rooftops... wild white waves surging over the rocks... It was beautiful, yet strange and rather scary.

"My brothers won't believe this," Rob said. "I've seen Embra from inside the royal castle. It's quite a place, isn't it?"

"Do you mean the city or the castle?"

"Both."

He sounded happier than before. It wasn't like Rob to be depressed for long.

"You know, this isn't the end of our journey," he said. "It's just the beginning, Jamie."

I felt a shiver run through me. Granny would have said it was caused by a rabbit running over the place where my grave would be. Rob thought I was cold and he closed the shutters.

I wasn't cold, though. I was afraid of what might lie ahead of us. And I was right to be afraid – although I couldn't even guess what was going to happen.

We didn't know that a Norse ship was approaching Embra harbour that very night, fighting against the gale. As for the city, with all its power and splendour – we didn't know about the darkness hidden at the heart of it, like rot inside an apple. Enemies outside, enemies inside... which would be worse?

But that's another story. As Rob said – we were just at the beginning.